A CHRISTMAS WISH

Samantha Baca

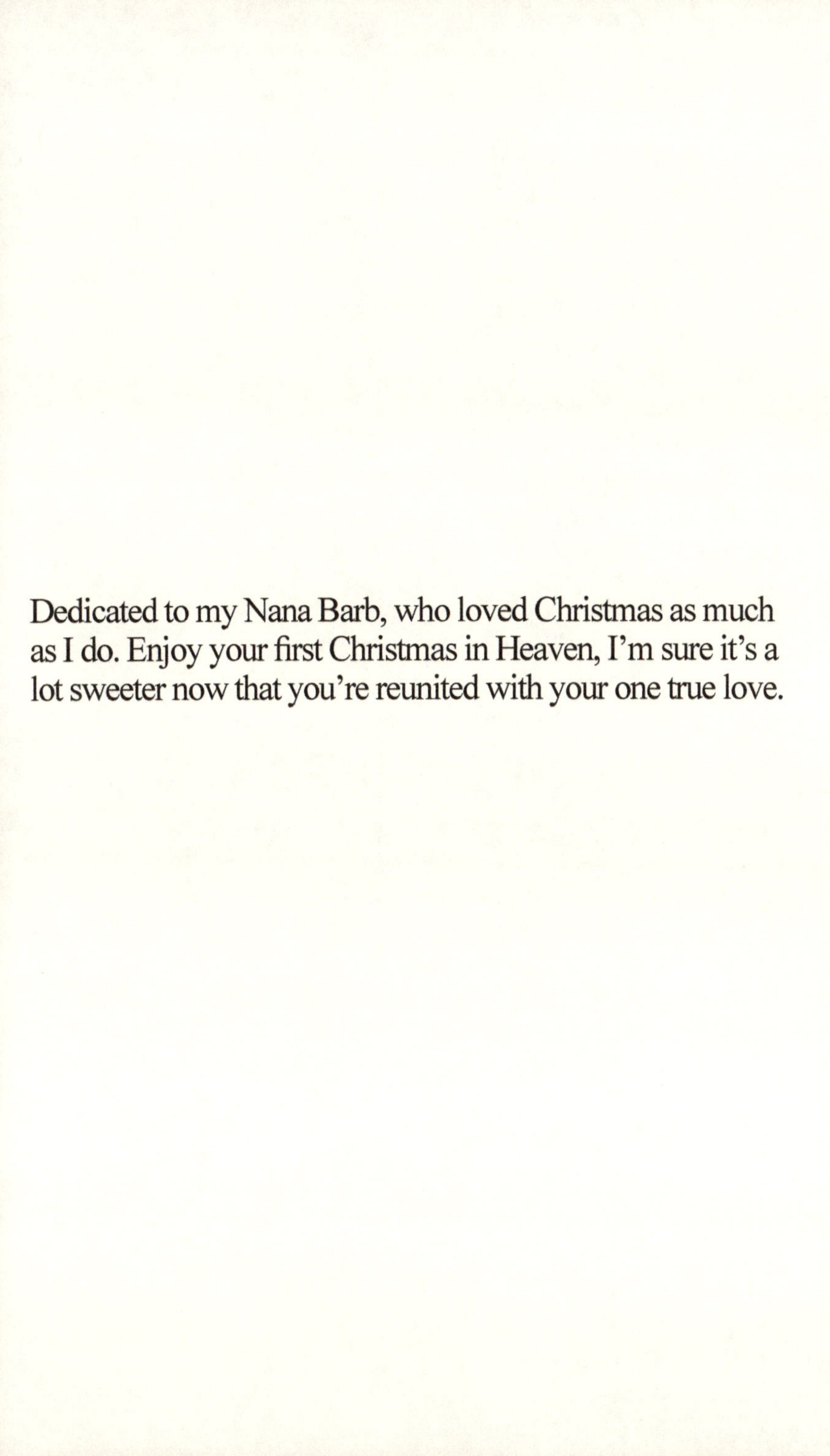

Dedicated to my Nana Barb, who loved Christmas as much as I do. Enjoy your first Christmas in Heaven, I'm sure it's a lot sweeter now that you're reunited with your one true love.

Contents

One

Everly

"Can I bring you another glass of wine?" the waiter asked, standing impatiently beside the table.

I glanced down at my phone, confirming that there were no new text messages or missed calls. It appeared I had been stood up. Again.

I searched the room for any sign of hope, spotting an attractive man waiting by the hostess station, a few feet away from me. It would be great if he was my blind date and maybe just hadn't seen me yet, but I already knew that I wouldn't be that lucky. IF my date did show up, I imagined it would either be some overly cocky douchebag who thought a $7.99 steak would get him into my pants or an inexperienced geek who had no idea what a clitoris was.

"I'm fine, thank you," I pushed out anxiously. "I'll wait until my—"

"Date arrives," he finished for me with a hint of snark. He rolled his eyes and trotted off to another table. That was the excuse I had been giving him for not ordering over the thirty minutes that I had been sitting there.

It was two weeks until Christmas, and every restaurant in Chicago had long wait times. I felt bad for tying up a table and keeping him from waiting on someone else that would order more than a house glass of wine, but, I was desperate to have my date show up. I didn't want to take any chances that they would after I left. I *needed* this more than I wanted to admit.

As I unlocked my phone and opened the text messages to *Brad*, if that was even his name, I heard someone walk over and stand by the table. My arms tingled with goosebumps, my fingers shaking slightly as I set my phone down. The excitement that he had finally shown up was quickly replaced with dread and anxiety when I noticed who was standing there instead.

"Hey, Everly," Tom said with a nod. His arm was wrapped around the rail-thin waist of his new girlfriend, who just so happened to be a model.

"Hey," I muttered, adjusting the linen napkin on my lap. I didn't bother to acknowledge her, just as she hadn't bothered to say anything to me.

"You here on a *date*?" he chuckled as if he couldn't believe it, nodding to the place setting beside me. "With your *boyfriend*?"

I looked around helplessly, praying that Brad would magically show up out of thin air.

"She's not here on a date," Staci said sarcastically. "Otherwise, she wouldn't be sitting here by herself, looking so sad and desperate. *If* she had a boyfriend, don't you think he'd be here by now?"

I bit my tongue, refusing to give her the satisfaction of getting a response to that.

"You're here *alone*? I didn't think you liked to eat by yourself," Tom noted.

"I don't," I bit out through gritted teeth. I wasn't going to let him get to me if I could help it, but *man,* if he didn't know how to push my buttons. I was also regretting telling him that I was dating someone since that lie seemed to be biting me in the ass at the moment.

I hadn't planned to make up such an elaborate story. When I saw him making out with Staci in his office after he emailed me that we needed to talk to, I panicked, and it just came rushing out. It was like the brain cells had magically disappeared and weren't allowing me to come up with actual words to reply with.

"So then you *are* waiting for someone. Did you get stood up?" His eyes lit up when he asked it as if it somehow gave him pleasure to see me so miserable.

"Obviously," Staci laughed, snorting in the process. She covered her mouth with a perfectly manicured hand and pretended to be embarrassed.

I was about to say something, though I had no idea what, when someone suddenly slid past Tom and Staci and stepped beside me.

"Hey, baby, sorry I'm late," he said loudly, bending down to kiss me as his warm hand softly tilted my chin up for my lips to meet his.

My eyes tried to focus on the handsome stranger from the hostess station before they fluttered shut with the kiss. His soft, full lips danced with mine as if they had done this a million times. It wasn't the awkward kind of first-date kiss that I was used to. It was the kind of kiss that sent shivers up my spine and sent heat rushing through my body at the promise of what else he could do with his tongue.

He pulled away and gave a tight smile to Tom and Staci as he sat down and placed the napkin in his lap.

Having noticed that someone else had *finally* sat down, the waiter approached our table, pen ready to start our order.

"I see that the rest of your party has arrived," he said shortly. "What may I get you to drink, sir?"

"Go ahead and bring us a bottle of whatever the lady is drinking."

The waiter nodded and walked off, tucking his notepad into the pocket of his apron.

"Well, I guess we should let you get to your dinner," Tom replied awkwardly, staring at the man next to me uneasily.

I simply nodded, glaring at Staci as her jaw stayed open while she stared in disbelief.

Tom nudged her before placing his hand on her lower back and leading her away from our table and out of the restaurant.

I placed both hands on the table in front of me and slowly released the breath I had been holding. I looked over and found dark hazel eyes locked onto me, studying me with curiosity.

"Thank you," I stammered, unsure of how to start. "I'm sorry about that."

"Don't be," he shrugged, getting situated in his seat. He

leaned back as the waiter grabbed the empty glass in front of him, filling it with water, then set it back on the table.

I waited until he left before I spoke again.

"Well, if you have somewhere else you need to be, please don't feel obligated to stay with me." I lifted my wine and took a drink.

"I don't have anywhere that I need to be," he answered with a grin that pulled up the corners of his mouth into a dazzling smile. "But if you'd rather that I go, I can."

I was too quick in my response, nearly knocking over my glass of water as my hand darted out to grab his wrist to keep him from moving. It was as if I was afraid that he would vanish into thin air as quickly as he had appeared.

"No," I said abruptly, my eyes wildly searching his. It felt like I was dreaming, and I wasn't ready to wake up.

"I mean, no, please stay," I added with a somewhat calmer breath. "I would love to treat you to dinner to say thank you for coming to my rescue."

"Thank you, but no," he started before we were interrupted again. He gave me a quick, tight smile before turning his attention away.

The waiter was back, this time with the bottle of wine and a basket of bread. This guy had *the worst* timing ever. He set the bread down and refilled my glass before pouring one for—whoever this guy was. I had kissed someone that I didn't even know his name.

"Are you ready to order?" he asked, pulling his notepad out of his pocket.

Mr. Sexy arched a brow at me, silently asking if I knew what I wanted. I felt my nerves running wild again, knowing that I would end up eating by myself after all. He had already declined my offer but didn't have enough time to get out of there before the waiter returned.

"I'll do the fettuccini with grilled chicken and a side salad," I answered.

"I'll do the same," he replied, sliding the menus back to the waiter. I wondered if maybe he was just being polite to keep from embarrassing me.

The waiter scribbled the information on the paper and grabbed the menus before rushing off.

"Thank you for the offer," he said once we were alone again. "But I will not let you pay for my meal."

I pulled my brows in. Out of the handful of dates that I had been on in the past few weeks, he was the first to object to me offering to pay for the meal. Not that I was in love with the idea of paying for every meal when I went on a date, but it was better than allowing some asshole to think that I owed him something because he paid. While it would be grand to simply split the ticket, I found that most of the *men* I had met weren't that open to the idea either.

"But, if you'll let me, I would love to treat you instead."

I laughed before I could stop myself. If I thought I was in a dream before, I was *definitely* in one now. Things like this *never* happened to girls like me. Hell, I don't think they happened to anyone who wasn't a paid actress in a rom-com movie.

"That's not necessary. Really."

Now it was his turn to frown at me.

"I would imagine that it's not *necessary*," he commented. "However, it would be my pleasure."

"Why are you being so nice to me?" I blurted out, tilting my head to the side. I was studying him like a foreign creature because that was exactly what it felt like he was.

"Why wouldn't I?"

"Because you don't even know me."

"And that's a reason *not* to be nice to you?"

"I've seen worse," I snorted, knowing it was the truth.

He pulled his lips into a thin smile and nodded.

"I'm Jared," he said, extending his hand to me.

I shook it, surprised by the softness.

"Everly."

"That's a beautiful name."

I tried to force down the butterflies that were fluttering in my stomach, impressed by his charm. There was no way that this was really happening. There had to be a catch. Maybe it was all a game, and I was on some reality TV show, like *Pranked*.

"Thank you," I said cautiously, not ready to let my guard down.

"You don't trust me, do you?" he asked, his grin pushing across his olive-toned skin. Suddenly, his eyes looked more green than brown with the way the light was hitting them. They were easy to get lost in.

"No," I laughed, leaning back in my seat. "I really don't."

"Why not?"

"Because you seem too good to be true."

"How so?" His lips curled up into a bigger smile as he seemed amused by my statement.

I took a few deep, steadying breaths before I answered.

"You popped up out of thin air, rescued me from an embarrassing situation with my ex-boyfriend, and you want to buy me dinner. Things like that don't just happen to me. So either I'm drunk," I glanced at what was left of my second glass of wine. "Or you are simply too good to be true. Maybe a figment of my imagination?"

He laughed, and it sounded like music to my ears. It was a deep laugh that made the tight muscles under his buttoned-up shirt move, drawing my eye as my fingers itched to trace the outline of each ridge.

"I can assure you that I'm real and that I just happened to be in the right place at the right time," he assured me.

"I find that hard to believe," I muttered.

"It's true," he chuckled with a wink. "I was at the hostess station, waiting to put in a to-go order when I overheard the conversation. I wasn't sure if someone else was going to show up, so I took a chance and decided to step in."

I felt my jaw drop open, partly embarrassed that he had heard our conversation and knew how pathetic I was, and somewhat impressed that he had wanted to help.

"No one deserves to be treated that way," he added. "I can't stand guys like that."

"Well, thank you. I don't think I'll ever find enough ways to show my gratitude to you for coming to my rescue."

"As I said, it's my pleasure."

The waiter returned with our plates and set them down in front of us. I took the opportunity to think about what he had said as we started to eat.

"So, you got stood up?" he asked, raising an eyebrow before taking a bite of fettuccine.

I nearly choked on my water, caught off guard by his question. I brought my napkin up and blotted my mouth.

"Yup," I said with a sigh as if I didn't care. The truth was that I did—a lot.

"It's his loss." He shrugged, his broad shoulders pulling tight against the thick fabric of his shirt.

I smiled but said nothing for a moment. I twirled noodles around my fork and then stopped.

"I would like to think so, but this is the third time in a week, so I'm starting to think that maybe it's me."

He set his fork down on his plate and lifted his glass to take a drink of wine.

"Why would you think that?"

"Well, there has to be a reason that I got stood up by three different guys in one week. That just seems like it has to be me. Maybe they walked in, saw me, and decided to leave."

"You had three dates with three different guys this week, and they all stood you up?"

I nodded, taking a bite to occupy my mouth, so I didn't say anything more embarrassing.

"Why so many dates?" he asked without any judgment in his tone.

I waited for the waiter to refill our glasses of water before I told him the depressing truth.

"My work is having a big, fancy holiday party this weekend, and I wanted—no, *needed* to find a date to go with me. I don't have much time to get out and socialize, so I had a few people set me up. This one was a blind date that my mother set up with some lady that goes to her church. She knew a young man who would be perfect for me." I laughed at how stupid everything sounded before I added, "I'm not sure if the guy even exists."

"Where is the party at?" he asked, ignoring everything else.

"Palmer House Hotel," I swallowed. "They've booked a ballroom for the party Saturday night, but they're also paying for a room for each employee. It's a formal event, and everyone is expected to stay the night since there's a mandatory brunch in the morning. I think they're bribing us with the party and beautiful room before they unload all of the work crap on us the next morning," I joked, starting to ramble.

He leaned back in his seat and pushed his plate away. A few seconds passed before he reached down and adjusted his black satin tie.

"I'll go with you," he offered, looking deep into my eyes.

I pulled my head back in surprise.

"You want to go to my holiday party with me?" I questioned.

"Sure," he said softly. "You need a date, and I'm free this weekend."

This all felt too good to be true. Just when I was starting to let my guard down and believe this could be real, I began to question everything all over again.

"There's another thing," I added hesitantly. "I kinda told them that I've been seeing someone. So they're going to expect that…." My voice trailed off, too embarrassed to complete the sentence.

"So, not only will I be your *date, but* I'll also be your…?"

"Boyfriend."

If he was the least bit uncomfortable with hearing any of this, he didn't let on. He stayed perfectly composed as he took a drink and then set his glass down.

"Okay," he said smoothly.

"Are you sure you want to do this?" I asked, ready for him to reconsider.

He laughed and nodded his head.

"Yeah, I'm sure. Besides, I have a favor that I'll need in return."

"Well, you've saved me a few times already, I'd be happy to help you however I can."

"Trust me, you might reconsider that once you know what it is." He laughed, sending a surge of nervousness through me as I wondered what I had just gotten myself into.

Two

Jared

The week dragged on, as I waited anxiously to pick Everly up Saturday night. I hadn't talked to her much since our unexpected dinner Tuesday night, but I sure as hell hadn't stopped thinking about her. We had texted a few times to confirm the details for tonight, but my head was distracted with thoughts of her brilliant blue eyes and wavy brown hair that hung right above her ass when she got up to leave.

Not only was I obsessing over seeing her again, but I also couldn't get that kiss out of my head. I had kissed what felt like hundreds of women in my lifetime—hell if I knew the actual number—but no one had ever kissed me like she had. There was this intense spark that ignited between us, and I was reluctant to pull away.

It was almost 6:30, and I was picking her up at 6:45. Maybe it was my excitement to see her, or perhaps I was just naturally an early person, but there I was, sitting outside in my truck, watching the clock on the dashboard, and counting down the minutes until I could see her.

I didn't want to look like a pervert stalking her from the street, so I turned up the radio and played on my phone, hoping to look busy.

A few minutes later, I saw her front door open as she peeked outside. I turned the truck off and climbed out, taking in how beautiful she looked. Her hair was pulled up tightly on her head with a few pieces that curled behind her ear. A long black dress wrapped tightly around her body and loosened enough at the bottom to allow her to walk in the thin black heels that she had on.

"You look beautiful," I stammered, as I walked up to her porch. She smiled nervously and ran a hand down her dress.

"Thank you," she said shyly. "You look very handsome."

I watched as she tried to check me out discreetly, her facial expressions giving her away as her eyes roamed over my body.

My suit was custom-tailored and fit like a glove. I wasn't sure what she would wear, so I stuck with the black one, knowing that I couldn't go wrong with that. My tie was black with shades of grey pinstripes that paired perfectly with the silver necklace that dipped into the cleavage of her strapless dress.

"You ready to go?" I asked, shoving my hands into my pockets to keep from touching her.

"Yeah, let me grab my coat and lock up real quick."

I stepped back, giving her some room as a gust of wind pushed past us, sending a chill through me.

A few minutes later, she was wearing a long, thick black peacoat with a small wallet-looking purse tucked beneath her arm and a small duffle bag on her shoulder. She locked the door and then turned to face me. I could tell that she was nervous as I extended my hand to help her down the few steps to the driveway. When she placed her hand in mine, I felt her skin's warmth and softness, which sent another chill down my spine.

I walked her to the truck, opened her door, and helped her inside before I rushed off to the driver's side to get in. Once the vehicle was started, I cranked up the heater, making sure it didn't blow her hair but kept her warm and toasty.

"Are you excited about tonight?" I asked casually, checking my rearview mirror as I made my way to the hotel.

"I'm not sure that excited is the right word," she laughed nervously.

"Why not?"

"I'm not a social person, so these types of things are not my favorite. And then I'm worried that..."

"That people will know that I'm not your boyfriend?" I finished for her. I needed to know where her head was before the night started so that I didn't make things worse for her.

"Yeah," she sighed. "I already know that they'll take one look at you and think that I paid you to be my date."

"Are you calling me a hooker?" I joked, giving her my best smile as I tried to calm her nerves.

I watched for a brief moment as the corners of her mouth tilted up into a smile.

"That's not what I meant," she giggled.

"Well, it worked out well for Julia Roberts in Pretty Woman," I offered, loving the way her smile pulled tighter across her face, lighting up her blue eyes. Unfortunately, it disappeared as quickly as it had appeared.

She stayed quiet, chewing her nail nervously and watched out the window as we got closer to the hotel. Once we were there, I parked and turned to look at her.

"Nothing bad is going to happen, Everly," I assured her. "I'm here as your date, as your *boyfriend*," I added. "I promise that you will not regret having me come with you and that all of your coworkers will believe that we're together by the end of the night."

She shifted uneasily in her seat, staring at someone ahead of us. I turned my attention to where she was looking and saw the same couple that had been at her table harassing her at the restaurant the other night.

"Umm, there's one more thing that I need to tell you," she said quietly, turning to look at me.

I slightly raised a brow and waited.

"The guy you met the other night—Tom. Well, he's my ex-boyfriend."

"Okay…." There was more to that story, I could just feel it.

"And he's also my boss."

I blew out a heavy breath. Things just got a hell of a lot more complicated really quick.

Three

Everly

I tried to get my legs to stop shaking as I got out of the truck and took Jared's hand. Why did I think it was a good idea to wear six-inch heels tonight? Besides the fact that they were the only shoes that were tall enough to keep my dress from pooling on the ground, I had a brief moment where I had wanted to impress Jared. Now I would be lucky if I could manage to walk in them without tripping and breaking my neck.

We were ushered inside and directed to the ballroom, where people were already mingling inside. I glanced around, trying to find where Tom and Staci had gone. Hopefully, they went up to their rooms to get situated. Of course it's what I should have done, but the thought of taking Jared up to my room sent butterflies through my stomach and made my palms sweat. Instead, I accepted the offer to have the bellhop take my bag up to my room for me.

Once inside the ballroom, I looked around to see if there was assigned seating—which there was. I groaned silently when I found my name on the list next to Tom's. It made sense that they would put each department together at their own table, but I hated the idea of having to sit next to him and spend the evening hearing Staci talk about how hard it was to be so beautiful and thin.

"Did you want something to drink?" Jared asked quietly in my ear as his hand rested lightly on my lower back.

It felt like he could sense how nervous I was. He gently led me over to the bar and kept his hand protectively on me as we ordered our drinks. The bartender was handsome but definitely out of my league as he tilted his head back and laughed at something the busty red-headed waitress said to him. It was hard to concentrate on any words coming out of her mouth when her shirt plunged so low that her breasts almost spilled over as she leaned up against the bar top.

He gave a quick nod to Jared before sliding our glasses over and moving on to the next couple who had walked up. Jared tucked some cash into the tip jar and picked up our drinks as we moved out of the way. He handed me my drink carefully before pulling a sip of beer out of the bottle his strong hand was wrapped around. I took a sip of my martini and let the alcohol kiss my tongue before making its way down my throat, spreading warmth and a sense of calm through me with each drink.

People were scattered around the room as it started to get more packed. There was a dance floor off to the side of the room and a band still setting up on the stage.

"Did you want to find our seats?" Jared suggested, likely seeing the look of dread on my face as I considered having to mingle with everyone.

"Yes, please."

We walked over to the tables and scanned them until we found table 17. I hoped that at least this part was open seating so we could sit next to anyone other than Tom and Staci.

"It looks like we're right here," Jared said, finding our name cards before I could.

I offered a tight smile when I saw Tom's name next to mine. Jared reached over and swapped our names, putting him next to Tom and me next to Susan, the older woman that I absolutely loved in our department.

We sat down, and I felt somewhat more comfortable than I had before. Soon, people started making their way to the tables, and I felt the dread piling up as Tom sat down next to Jared with an audible grunt of disgust.

Without warning, Jared reached up and wrapped his arms casually around my shoulders as if this was the most natural thing in the world. Instead of wanting to pull away from his touch, I found it so comforting that I wanted to lean closer to him and feel the warmth of his body next to mine.

"You again," Tom stated curtly, turning to look at Jared. Since the table was round, I still had a good view of him and Staci as they sat there, staring in disbelief at Jared sitting next to me.

When Jared didn't respond, Tom leaned forward and caught my eye.

"I thought you were coming by yourself?" he asked sharply.

"I told Gail that I was bringing a date when I RSVP'd for two on the form."

Gail was the director of human resources and was responsible for putting together the holiday party. I had given her my form after my fingers trembled when marking the box for two. I had no idea who I was bringing with me and panicked that I would have to pay for dinner for the date that didn't show up. I was desperate to prove to Tom that I had moved on, even if that meant I had to fake a boyfriend at this stupid party. Especially since I had opened my stupid big mouth and told him that I had one.

"Well, she didn't tell me," he scoffed, unfolding the napkin that was resting on his plate.

"Why would she tell you?" I asked, pulling my brows tightly together as I leaned forward. I felt Jared's fingers lightly caress my skin above my dress and started to relax again.

"Because it's *my* department. I should know who's coming."

"You knew that I was coming. Whether or not I brought a date was none of your damn business."

"What you do is my business, Everly," he bit out. "I worry about you and whoever *this* is."

I felt Jared's body stiffen beside me and knew that Tom had struck a nerve.

"As I said, that is none of your business. So stop acting like it is and worry about your girlfriend flirting with the waiter." I nodded at Staci, who was oblivious to our conversation as she was turned all the way around in her chair, twirling her hair on her finger as she giggled shamelessly with the waiter beside her.

I reached forward and grabbed the heavy glass filled with ice water and brought it to my lips, trying to steady my hand enough to take a drink.

Jared leaned in closer, and I felt his breath hot on my neck as he spoke.

"Do you trust me?" he asked quietly.

I nodded, my blood still boiling from Tom.

He leaned back in his seat and lowered his arm from around my shoulders, resting his hand on my thigh.

I gasped from the touch, nearly spilling my glass of water. Tom's eyes darted over to us; his features pinched in annoyance on his face.

I set the glass down gently and shyly looked away from Susan as she eyed me cautiously to see if I was okay.

I heard a low chuckle from Jared as his hand gently squeezed my thigh. I looked up at him and saw a mischievous smile on his face as he winked.

He was so drop-dead sexy that for a moment, I forgot anyone else was in the room with us. I pulled in a slow, deep breath, remembering the way his lips had felt against mine the other night. I had no idea what to expect tonight with him pretending to be my boyfriend, but part of me desperately hoped that it meant that he would kiss me again. Maybe even more.

It had been a long time—a really, *really* long time—since I had felt a man's hands on my body, even longer since I had someone make love to me and not rush through it. Aside from my vibrator, I couldn't remember when someone else had given me an orgasm. My love life was as depressing and even more pathetic than my social life.

The waitstaff moved around the room quickly, placing baskets of bread and butter on the tables and refilling the glasses of water and tea. Jared leaned back as they refilled his water, adding more ice to the glass in the process.

When no one was looking, he dipped a finger in and pulled out an ice cube before putting it in his mouth. The next thing I knew, he was leaning closer to me, gently running his tongue along my neck as the ice melted around it. I closed my eyes and tilted my head to the side, giving him more access.

My heart was racing from the thrill of it. The cold of the ice paired with the heat from his tongue sent my body into overdrive as my senses were pushed to full alert. I wanted to reach over and grab him, pull him closer to me as we forgot about everyone and everything in this room.

"You make it really easy to pretend to be your boyfriend," he whispered in my ear before gently nipping at my earlobe.

"You're better than any boyfriend I've had before," I muttered, digging my fingers into my thighs as I tried to keep from moaning.

"Then you haven't been with the right guy," he added, slowly pulling away.

His eyes were a darker shade of green than they were a few minutes ago, and I could tell that this had affected him as much as it did me. He sat up straight in his chair and acted like he hadn't just tortured me with his skilled tongue.

Soon they were serving dinner, and we were distracted by our food. I speared a piece of asparagus with my fork and brought it to my lips, pausing when I noticed Jared watching me. My lips were parted, ready to take a bite.

"Lucky asparagus," he muttered with a grin before focusing on his salmon.

I felt the blush pinch my cheeks as I took a bite and tried not to choke on it. He knew all of the right things to say and do to make me feel sexy and seen—something I hadn't had in a long time.

After dinner, they cleared our plates and served dessert and coffee. I was already full, but the molten chocolate cake with vanilla ice cream was calling my name.

"This cake looks as good as you," Jared commented, loud enough to earn an eye roll from Tom. I knew he was doing it on purpose, just to get a rise out of him, but there was something about how he said it that almost had me believing it.

"Thank you," I said, suddenly feeling brave. I dug my spoon in, grabbing a bit of chocolate cake and ice cream, and turned to Jared. "Wanna see how good it tastes?"

I knew my choice of words would send a clear note to Tom that I wasn't talking about the cake. I held the spoon steadily as Jared leaned forward and wrapped his mouth around it, slowly pulling the contents off before licking his lips.

He studied me as he chewed, his eyes never leaving mine. His finger reached up and gently wiped the sides of his mouth before he spoke.

"That cake is delicious," he answered sexily. "But you taste better."

I felt my cheeks burn red with embarrassment. Tom scoffed beside him, tossing his spoon onto his plate and shoving it away. What did he have to be angry about? In the five years we were together, he had maybe gone down on me one or two times, using it as his birthday gift to me when he forgot to purchase a real gift.

"So dear, how long have you two been together?" Susan asked, turning her attention to us. She had obviously missed the dirty part of the conversation.

"Four months," I said at the same time that Jared said, "Six months."

She looked between us, confused by our answers. I laughed nervously, not sure what to say. Jared wrapped his arm around my shoulders again, this time pulling me into his body as he hugged me and planted a kiss on my temple.

"She counts the day that she officially said yes to being my girlfriend. I count the day that I first started chasing her. She put up a hard fight, but in the end, I won her love and made her mine."

Susan held her hand to her heart and looked warmly at us.

"That's so sweet," she sighed. "It's good that you found someone willing to chase after you," she said, giving a dirty look to Tom as she looked past Jared. "You look really happy, dear. I'm glad you found someone who clearly worships you the way you deserve."

"There's not a thing in this world that I wouldn't do for her," Jared replied casually. "Especially knowing how much she's been through already, I'm more than ready to show her what a real man can do for her. And *to* her," he said quietly in my ear.

Tom excused himself and went to the bathroom while Staci ventured off to the dance floor. I was tired and had enough socializing already. I wanted nothing more than to leave and head on up to my room, but I wasn't sure I was ready to say goodbye to Jared. While we had talked a few times since dinner, we hadn't discussed whether he was planning to stay the night with me or attend brunch in the morning. Since I knew my luck was coming to an end soon, I assumed he would leave and go on his way as soon as it was safe to do so. Hell, he probably had another date lined up after with some beautiful woman who would reap the benefits of the things he had been whispering in my ear all night.

An hour later, everyone started making their way to their rooms, and I knew it was time to do the same.

"Everly, I'm so glad you made it," Gail said over my shoulder as she came over to our table. "I'm sorry I didn't get over here earlier to say hi. It's been nonstop from the moment I got here."

"No worries," I replied with a smile.

"I don't think we've met," Gail said to Jared, reaching over to extend her hand to him. "I'm Gail."

"Jared," he replied, shaking her hand.

"It's nice to meet you." She smiled and looked past him as someone called her name. "I look forward to seeing you at brunch in the morning. You two enjoy your stay tonight."

She gently squeezed my shoulder before rushing off to tend to someone else.

I had thought—no, hoped—that Tom had left when I hadn't seen him for a while. So it was an unpleasant surprise when he spoke over my shoulder.

"He's staying the night with you?" he asked bitterly.

Before I could answer, Jared wrapped an arm around my waist and pulled me into him.

"How else am I going to make sure she stays warm tonight?" He gave him a smug smile and started to lead me away.

Then, at the last minute, I turned and looked over my shoulder at Tom, who was still watching us. "Oh, and don't worry if you hear me screaming. That's just what I sound like when I'm not *faking* an orgasm," I said with more confidence than I ever knew I had.

My heart was racing when I spun back around and leaned into Jared as his fingers dug lightly into my side. He chuckled as we walked away, leaving Tom in stunned silence as Staci muttered under her breath about me being a lucky bitch.

Four

Jared

It didn't go unnoticed that Everly's fingers trembled as she tried to stick the card into the key reader.

"Here, let me," I offered, placing my hand over hers and sliding the card away from her. She smiled and stepped out of the way as I reached forward and swiped the card, opening the door.

I held it open as she walked in and looked around. The room was beautiful with a king-sized bed centered in the middle of it. There wasn't much else in the room other than a dresser with a tv sitting on top of it, a small table with two chairs by the window, and two nightstands on each side of the bed.

"Thank you for walking me up," she said nervously. "Please don't feel obligated to stay."

She was still standing in the same spot, fidgeting with her purse as she watched me. There was something about the way that she was looking at me that said that she didn't want me to go.

"Do you want me to leave?" I asked gently, giving her plenty of space so I didn't crowd her.

"Do you want to?" She raised her eyebrows as she waited anxiously.

"No."

Her chest rose and fell as she let out a jagged breath.

"I don't want you to go either."

I watched her as she looked around, unsure of herself and her decision.

"If you change your mind, just let me know. I don't want to make you uncomfortable."

She tipped her head back and laughed. A genuine laugh that made her eyes crinkle in the corners.

"Uncomfortable is the last thing I would use to describe how you make me feel."

My eyebrows shot up, surprised by this revelation. I knew that she had been receptive to my touch earlier, and I had noticed how she blushed with the things that I said, but I wasn't sure how much of it was a show for Tom and how much she was genuinely reacting to me.

I took a few steps toward her, gauging her reaction along the way.

"How do I make you feel?" I asked once I was standing in front of her.

She chewed her bottom lip before answering.

"Sexy. Wanted. Nervous."

I reached up and gently caressed her cheek with my thumb.

"Why do you say it like it's a bad thing?" I chuckled.

Her hand reached up and held onto my hand as she closed her eyes.

"Because," she breathed heavily. "I haven't felt this turned on by a man in years, and you barely touched me. It's embarrassing."

I lifted her chin with my finger and waited for her to open her eyes and look at me.

"There's nothing embarrassing about that, Everly. And anyone who tells you otherwise has no idea what they're talking about. You're a beautiful woman who deserves to be touched in a way that makes you feel sexy and wanted."

Her blue eyes locked onto mine, and I noticed the lust simmering beneath.

"How are you so perfect?" she asked, tilting her head to the side. "You know all of the right things to say to make me feel calm when I would normally be freaking out."

"I'm not perfect," I laughed, letting my hand drop from her face. "I'm far from it. But I would like to think that I'm a fairly observant person. Plus, I'm an expert at body language."

I shrugged cockily, earning a laugh from her.

"You're an expert at body language?" she asked, shifting her weight to the other leg and folding her arms across her chest.

Her body was turned toward me with the slit in her dress pulling tight on the leg closest to me.

"I am," I assured her, noting all of the things she was subconsciously saying.

"Okay, then what is mine saying?" She licked her lips before pulling her bottom one in between her teeth.

I made an effort to study her, looking her up and down painfully slow as she squirmed beneath my stare.

Finally, I said, "that you want me."

She let out a small gasp and sucked in a breath.

"The way that you're standing, with your feet slightly spread in a way that makes the slit pull tighter across your thigh. And the way that you have your arms folded, pressing your breasts up so they're on display for me. Both of those confirm that you want me to see your body. But, aside from those, it's the little things. Like the way your breathing has changed or how your eyes have darkened because you're aroused." I stepped closer to her, our bodies nearly touching each other. "I bet if I were to slip a finger inside, I would find out how wet you are."

Her breath caught in her throat as she listened to the words I said. She was so beautiful, and I couldn't stop thinking about how much I wanted her.

"Make a Christmas wish, and I'll make it come true," I coaxed.

"I don't know what to say," she whispered shakily, looking down at her feet.

"Tell me what you want," I pleaded, as I watched the blush creep up her neck.

She chewed her bottom lip before looking into my eyes.

"You," she breathed.

Five

Everly

I tried to act cool and collected as I stood there, watching Jared's eyes scan my face. I knew that he was overly observant, but I didn't know if he knew just how nervous he made me.

I waited, hoping that he would take me at my word and have his way with me. Even though I was scared shitless of that actually happening, a big part of me wished it would. What I would give to just feel careless and free for one night as I enjoyed whatever pleasures he gave to me.

The longer he stayed quiet, the more I worried about what he would say when he finally spoke. The silence between us was deafening.

Panic started to rise within me, my palms sweating as I shifted, praying that my heels wouldn't choose this moment to give in and break. That would be one hell of a way to go.

"I should get going," he said quietly, a hint of disappointment in his voice.

I felt the air rush out of me, along with the hopes I had been holding onto.

"Oh, okay." I frowned and tried to shake off the feeling of rejection that was sitting so heavily on my shoulders.

I stepped back, allowing him to walk past me as he gently slid his hand across my stomach in the process.

"Did I do something wrong?" I blurted out. I had faced a lot of rejection lately, so this time I wanted to hear why he was leaving. If there was something that I was doing that was driving men away, I needed to know what it was.

He stopped and looked at me.

"No, Everly. You didn't do anything wrong."

"Then why are you leaving?" I was so confused and had no idea what had caused the sudden change between us.

"Because," he sighed and scrubbed a hand down his face. "When you said that you wanted me, your body language said otherwise."

"I meant what I said," I objected.

He dropped his hand and grabbed mine.

"Your body said otherwise," he explained. "Your words said that was what you wanted, but the way your shoulders tightened and you flinched at them said otherwise. And that's okay, Everly. There's nothing wrong with listening to your instincts."

I was frustrated with myself, and I could see that he knew it. I wanted to tear down the walls I had worked so hard to build up and let him in, but I couldn't. Thanks to Tom, I found it nearly impossible to let anyone in.

"You don't have to go," I said easily. "I mean, obviously, we're not going to do anything, but you can hang out for a bit if you want to."

Even though I knew that nothing more would happen between us, I was reluctant to have him leave. Maybe it was me being selfish, but I didn't want to be alone tonight. The few hours we had spent together had been different than I had expected, and I wasn't ready for it to end. Not only did I feel comfortable around him, I felt safe. Even if I couldn't get myself to jump his bones like I wanted to, I didn't want him to leave.

"Sure," he replied with a smile. "Do you want to watch some tv or find a movie?"

I nodded, feeling somewhat relieved that he wasn't rushing off now that he knew he wasn't going to get any. *That was a change.*

"I need to change real quick," I said, eager to get out of my dress and into something more comfortable. "Sorry, I would offer you something to wear, but I only brought a pair of pajamas and clothes for tomorrow."

"It's okay," he laughed. "I wasn't sure what the plan was, so I went ahead and packed a bag just in case. Go ahead and get changed, and I'll run down and grab it real quick."

"Okay," I agreed. "Go ahead and take the room key so you can let yourself in while I get situated."

He smiled and took it, then he was out the door and gone. I let out a heavy sigh as I tried to process everything that had happened tonight. I grabbed my bag from the floor and went to the bathroom to get changed.

It felt nice to take my hair down. Each bobby pin that I pulled out relieved some of the tension and pressure on my head until they were finally out. I ran my hands through my hair, trying to smooth out the tangles.

My eyes hurt from the makeup I was wearing, and I was desperate to take it off. I rarely wore makeup, and when I did, it usually bothered my eyes. Knowing that I didn't have to impress Jared since we weren't planning to sleep together, I decided to go ahead and wash it off. I dried my face with the hand towel hanging on the bar beside me and then brushed my teeth. Just because we weren't having sex didn't mean that we wouldn't kiss. It was better to be prepared, just in case.

I hung my dress over the rod in the shower, not bothering to go out and search for one in the closet by the door. Unfortunately, I hadn't packed for tonight with the idea that Jared would be hanging out with me. It seemed too good to be true, so I had dismissed the thought and packed to stay by myself. I glanced nervously in the mirror at my booty shorts and cropped sweatshirt. It's what I would wear to bed any other night when I was at home by myself, but it felt slightly sexy and inappropriate now. The only other clothes I had with me were the jeans and sweater I had packed for tomorrow.

Deciding that there weren't any other choices, I sighed and slid my duffle bag under the counter before opening the door and walking into the room. I stopped in my tracks, my jaw dropping open when I saw Jared changing.

Gray sweatpants hung low on his hips, and the muscles in his torso were on full display as he lifted his arms to pull his t-shirt over his head.

There wasn't an ounce of fat on his toned body that looked like it belonged on the cover of a magazine. I tried to swallow, but my throat was suddenly dry. Instead, I just stood there, drinking him in like I was stranded in the desert, and he was the last drop of water.

He finished pulling it over his head and turned toward me once he realized that I was standing there. The shirt slowly fell, covering my perfect view.

"Sorry, I thought I could change before you came out," he apologized.

"Don't be sorry," I stammered, trying to force words out past the dryness in my throat.

"Do you want me to run down and see if they have an ice machine?" he offered.

I tried to focus on what he was asking, but the only thing I could think about was the way he made my skin feel earlier when he trailed his tongue along it with the ice cube in his mouth.

His lips turned up into a sexy smile, and his eyes lit up as he walked closer to me. It was as if he was reading every dirty thought I was having.

"Are you okay?" he asked playfully, lifting my chin with his fingers. My eyes locked onto his, and I felt a pull deep inside that made me want to jump into his arms and ride him into the sunset.

"Yes," I whispered.

"So, do you want me to?"

"Want you to what?"

"Get ice," he said slowly. My eyes drifted down to his lips as he licked them when he spoke.

"Ice," I repeated breathlessly. My chest rose and fell heavily as I stood there, hypnotized by him.

"Ice," he confirmed, lowering his mouth to mine. He kissed me softly as his hands slid down and wrapped around my waist. I moaned at the contact and felt my legs start to give. I knew what my body wanted, even if my head kept getting in the way.

After a few minutes, he pulled away, breaking the kiss. I could feel his erection through his pants and knew that he was as turned on as I was. I was practically panting, wanting more.

"I can go get some ice," he stammered breathlessly. "And some bottles of water."

I rubbed at my lips, missing the feeling of his against mine.

"Okay, thank you."

He pulled away and walked out the door, leaving me there in a confused state of bliss.

Ten minutes later, he was back with a bucket of ice, a few bottles of water, and a random assortment of snacks. I was cuddled in the bed, under the covers, after feeling self-conscious about what I was wearing when he walked in.

"Do you want snacks in bed?" he asked, kicking his shoes off and leaving them under the table by the window. He set the ice bucket down and went to the mini coffee bar by the door to bring over two glasses.

"Sure, thank you." I scooted over, giving him room to climb in next to me when he was ready.

He handed me a glass filled with ice, then tossed the pile of snacks onto the bed beside me. I was surprised by how comfortable I felt with him there, moving around me as if we had done this a thousand times. Finally, once he had everything situated, he climbed onto the bed and sat beside me on top of the covers.

It was cold, even with the heater on.

"You can get under the covers if you want," I offered, hoping not to sound too desperate.

"I'm good, thanks," he said and turned his attention to the bag of Fritos in his hand.

I wasn't sure how to take it, so I turned my attention to the tv and pretended to look for something to watch.

"What do you want to watch?" I asked.

"I'm fine with whatever you want to watch."

I kept flipping through the channels and finally decided on an old action movie. I tried to get comfortable but couldn't. As I squirmed around, I couldn't help but wonder what he was thinking and why he was being so nice to me.

We sat there quietly, watching the movie and eating snacks for a while before I let out a heavy sigh. He turned to look at me, his head tilted in question.

"Everything okay?" he asked.

"Yeah," I sighed. "I'm fine."

I pulled my lower lip in between my teeth and turned my attention back to the tv.

"You're a terrible liar," he noted, turning on his side and resting on his elbow as he faced me. "What's wrong?"

"Nothing. Really."

He reached over and grabbed the remote sitting in between us, turning the tv off so I would have to stop pretending to watch it.

"Everly, talk to me."

"There's nothing to talk about," I laughed, trying to make light of the situation.

"Remember what I said earlier about being able to read your body language?"

I took a deep breath and slowly let it out.

After a few minutes, I finally gave in.

"I'm just feeling confused, and it's frustrating."

"What do you mean?" he asked, sitting up and turning all the way to look at me.

"I know that you're here, pretending to be my boyfriend for the party, but I can't help but feel like there's something more going on. Like when we kissed a little bit ago. I felt something, and it *seemed* like maybe you did too. But now it's like nothing happened, and you're staying far away from me like I have cooties or something. I mean, you won't even get under the covers with me, and it's freezing in here."

"The reason that I haven't pushed any further is because I respect you, Everly. There is nothing—and I mean *nothing*—that I want more than to strip you down and devour every inch of your body. To hear you scream my name over and over as you come undone and climax for everyone to hear. I didn't want to get under the covers with you because I don't trust myself enough to keep my hands to myself. I don't want to risk the temptation."

"But I'm sitting here saying that it's okay. You don't have to avoid the temptation," I insisted, suddenly hating how desperate I sounded.

"Trust me," he sighed, leaning forward to run his thumb along my cheek. "I do. Because if I don't, you'll end up regretting it in the morning, and I can't stand the thought of that. But if you're worried that I don't find you attractive, I can tell you with 100% certainty that I would love nothing more than to be inside of you right now, Everly. That's *my* Christmas wish. But not tonight."

He picked the remote up and turned the tv back on, acting as if nothing had just happened.

Six

Jared

The sun peeked through the curtains, spreading a warm glow on the wall behind me. I rolled over and looked at Everly, who was still sound asleep beside me. Her hair was fanned out beneath her in soft waves, making her look like an angel.

I hadn't expected to stay the night with her and couldn't remember what time we had finally fallen asleep. I tried to get up and sneak out of the room after she had started snoring, but she reached out and grabbed my arm, holding me in place. I decided to wait a little longer and then try again, but instead, I fell asleep.

I planned to sneak off last night, go home and get some sleep—after dealing with my massive erection in the shower—then come back and go to brunch with her so she didn't have to go by herself. More so, I didn't want Tom to know that I hadn't stayed the night with her after all.

I rolled out of bed and quietly stood up, stretching to wake myself up. I closed my eyes and reached higher, feeling my shirt pull up in the process as my sweats shifted lower. When I lowered my arms and opened my eyes, I found Everly awake, watching me.

I hated seeing the lust in her eyes and knowing that there was nothing that I could do about it. Not right now, anyway.

"Good morning," I said, smiling at her.

"Good morning," she replied, her eyes moving back up my body to my face. "Did you sleep okay?"

"Yeah, I'm a little sore, but I'm okay." I rubbed a hand along the back of my neck, feeling how stiff it was from sleeping in an odd position.

"I'm sorry," she apologized, propping herself up on her arm. "A hot shower might help," she suggested.

I felt the strain against my briefs and knew that a cold shower would be more appropriate right now.

"No need to be," I assured her. "I didn't plan to stay the night. I think I just got too comfortable and fell asleep."

"We both did," she laughed. "At one point, I woke up to you cuddling my breasts."

I closed my eyes and ran a hand through my hair.

"I'm so sorry," I apologized, embarrassed that I couldn't even keep my hands to myself in my sleep.

"It's okay," she giggled, pulling the sheets up to her chin. "I didn't mind. It helped my dreams get a little more *intense*."

Something flashed across her face that was a mix of embarrassment and lust, all mixed into one.

"Now I wanna know about this dream," I said, crossing my arms over my chest and watching her.

She covered her face with her arms and groaned, complaining that it was too embarrassing.

"Nope," I said with too much enthusiasm. "I wanna hear about it. Remember, you owe me?"

"That's the favor that you're cashing in on?" she questioned, keeping the sheet pulled up to her chin.

"One of many."

She narrowed her eyes at me and pretended to frown. She was absolutely adorable.

"Now spill it."

She looked away, slipping further under the covers.

"I will come in there and tickle you until you tell me," I warned.

She stopped wiggling and looked at me.

"You wouldn't."

I lifted a brow in response.

"Fine," she sighed and puffed a breath of air up, forcing her hair out of her face. "In my dream, we were *doing stuff.* And then I guess my body started to react to you caressing my breasts and I…. you know…." She trailed off, leaving her sentence to wrap around my mind in the dirtiest of ways.

"You had an orgasm?" I asked, intently focusing on her face as the red crept across it.

She nodded and pulled the covers over her head again.

"Wow," I said, sitting down on the edge of the bed with my

back slightly turned toward her.

"I know, I know," she whined. "I'm sorry. It's so embarrassing."

I looked over my shoulder and caught her eye.

"It's fucking hot as hell. I just wish I was awake to see it."

We were both quiet for a few moments before she scooted up and out of bed.

"I should probably get ready. Brunch is in an hour."

I nodded, wanting to volunteer that we take a shower together but kept my mouth shut instead. As she walked to the bathroom, I caught a quick glimpse of her and her ass that was barely covered by her shorts. I groaned as my dick pressed harder against my briefs. Today was going to be a *hard* day.

Seven

Everly

I ran my brush through my hair one last time and tried not to stare at Jared's reflection in the mirror behind me as he stripped down to jump in the shower. While he may not have had any intention of *stripping down,* he had taken his shirt off, and his sweatpants were hanging low enough to provoke dirty thoughts about what I wish would happen next.

I had thrown on my pajamas after I got out of the shower because I couldn't stand the thought of pulling on jeans or a tight sweater when my body was still damp. If I were at home, I would just get ready in my towel until I was completely dry, but I wasn't at home.

Once I heard the bathroom door close and the shower turn on, I took the opportunity to get dressed. I pulled my shirt up and over my head, tossing it onto the bed before hooking my fingers into the waistband of my shorts and pulling them down.

I was bent over, ass in the air, as I stepped out of them when I heard the bathroom door open. I didn't have time to cover up before I whipped around, surprising him with my bare breasts as much as he had surprised me.

His eyes widened as he took me in. I brought a hand up to try to cover my chest while moving my legs awkwardly to try to cover myself. I hadn't thought it was necessary to put underwear on since I wasn't getting dressed yet.

"Sorry," he coughed out as he swallowed hard. "I forgot to grab my clothes." He nodded to the change of clothes he had pulled out of his bag.

I nodded and pinched my eyes closed, hoping that I would disappear.

I heard him move past me, then rush back into the bathroom, closing the door behind him once again.

The air rushed out of my lungs quickly, pushing through my lips that were trembling.

Did that just happen?!

I didn't waste any time getting dressed after that. By the time he was done, I was sitting on the bed—fully clothed— pretending to look at something on my phone. Instead, I was obsessing over the fact that he had seen me naked, and there was nothing I could do about it.

"What time does brunch start?" he asked as he approached the bed, rolling his sleeves up. He looked more casual in a dark buttoned-down shirt and dark jeans.

"At eleven," I confirmed, scooting off the bed. I stood up, feeling awkward that he had seen me naked. "If you've changed your mind, you don't have to go."

He reached over to the table where his stuff was and picked up a black metal watch, clasping it around his wrist as he eyed me suspiciously.

"Do you not want me to go?"

I swallowed hard, trying to get past the dryness in my throat.

"No, it's not that," I whispered, unable to look at him.

He let out a soft whistle and took a few steps until he was right in front of me. Gently he cupped the side of my face, lifting it so I would have to look at him.

"I don't know how many times I have to tell you this, but I'll say it again." His voice was as smooth and velvety as his touch. "You have *nothing* to be embarrassed about. I'm sorry that I accidentally walked in on you, but I'm not sorry about what I saw."

My skin prickled as the heat washed over it, making me suddenly uncomfortable as my heart started beating hard against my chest.

"It took everything that I had to walk back into the bathroom and not rush over to touch you."

"Why didn't you?" I asked, nearly panting.

He chewed his bottom lip for a brief second before saying, "because I respect you. If anything happens between us, I want to make sure that you're fully on board."

I nodded, unable to say anything as I stared into his eyes. It amazed me how much they changed color, and I found myself wanting to get lost in the sea of green that was hypnotizing me.

"We should get going, so we're not late," he said as if he hadn't just melted my insides.

I stepped away from his touch and searched the room,

making sure I had packed up everything I had brought. We made our way down to his truck to drop off our bags before heading to brunch.

Brunch was in the same room as the night before, but this time it was decorated with a more festive theme and not the overly elegant feel it had last night. A giant Christmas tree adorned with colorful lights and ornaments stood in the center of the stage where the band had played. Beneath it were several wrapped gifts, begging to be opened. It was hard to believe that they had transformed the room so quickly.

I smiled and looked around, feeling more comfortable with the over-the-top Christmas decorations than I had last night when everything was elegant and formal. Jared and I found seats at the table in the far corner of the room. Thankfully there wasn't assigned seating this time, and everyone was free to sit wherever they wanted.

The noise grew louder as more people packed in and took their seats. Everyone was a mix of comfy and casual, which made me feel better about wearing jeans and a sweater.

Once everyone was seated, Gail made her way to the front of the room and took the microphone handed to her by one of the hotel employees.

"Good morning! First, I would like to thank all of you for attending, and I hope you had a fun time at the party last night and are well rested this morning! The fun isn't over yet," she warned, shaking her finger at the few people who groaned and hung their heads, their hangovers on full display.

"While we wait for the food to be served, I thought we could play a quick game." She waited and looked around the room, trying to find someone as excited about it as she was. "I mean, personally, I *love* games. But you know what I love even more?" She lowered the microphone and scanned the room. "Prizes."

She looked over her shoulder at the wrapped gifts under the tree.

"You don't *have* to participate in the games that we're going to play today, but I can guarantee you that there are some *fabulous* prizes to be won."

I felt Jared's fingers as they gently squeezed my knee. I looked up at him and received a wink before he nodded to Gail and the pile of presents behind her.

"The first game that we have is Christmas Tie. This will be done with teams of two. You don't need anything but a tie, and if you don't have one, there are a few that were left behind last night that you can use. Come on up, and let's get started." She stepped to the side and waved for everyone to join her.

"Do you wanna go?" Jared asked, low in my ear.

I looked around, unsure about it since I didn't love being the center of attention. I felt eyes on me and scanned the room, finding Tom in the corner, glaring at us.

Pulling my shoulders back and letting out a heavy breath, I turned to Jared and smiled.

"Sure, let's go."

We made our way up to the front of the room with the few other people who had decided to participate. It was an even number of males and females as everyone partnered up with someone of the opposite sex.

"Oh shoot, we don't have a tie," I whispered to Jared.

He smiled and reached into his pocket, pulling the one from last night out.

"I forgot to pack it earlier, so I just tucked it in my pocket. Guess that came in handy," he shrugged.

I smiled back and tried to shake off the nerves of having everyone—including Tom—watching us.

"Okay, so the way this will work is one person will use only one hand to tie their partner's tie. The first one done wins," Gail explained.

I wiggled my fingers, anxious to get started. I had tied my dad's tie for him thousands of times as I grew up so I could do this with my eyes closed.

"Since I imagine that most of these ladies have helped tie a tie before, we're going to switch it up and make it a little harder. These are some awesome prizes up for grabs, so we have to make you guys work for them. The first man who can successfully tie his partner's tie using only one hand will be our winner."

I looked at Jared and noticed a smirk flash across his face.

"Can we use other body parts?" Leroy from accounting asked, his brows pulled together in doubt as he studied the tie in his hand.

"You can use whatever body part you want to—as long as it's not your other hand or anything that will go against our handbook—let's keep it clean," she joked.

We all got into position, lining up in front of her with the women on one side and the men on the other. Gail counted to three and then instructed everyone to begin.

Jared kept his left hand tucked behind his back as he stepped closer and held the tie in his mouth as he used his right hand to brush my hair over my shoulder. I felt my heartbeat start to quicken from the warmth of his body as he gently placed the tie around my neck and pulled it to where he wanted it.

His brows were pinched together as he concentrated, and I found it hard to look away. I studied his features as he worked, noticing the light brown specks that complimented the green in his eyes.

"I'm going to lean in to try to tie this, but you have to stay still and don't squirm," he said, raising an eyebrow as if he didn't trust me.

I nodded and pulled my shoulders down to elongate my neck to give him more room to work. He leaned in and tilted his head to the side, his lips grazing my neck as his teeth bit onto the silk of the tie and pulled it. His breath was hot against my skin as his hand trailed across my collarbone, finding the other end of the fabric.

I felt paralyzed at that moment, afraid to move and lose his touch. My body reacted in ways that I didn't need my coworkers to see, but I couldn't stop it if I tried.

"Are you okay?" he whispered around the piece of fabric in his mouth.

"Yeah," I managed to breathe out, staying completely still.

He tilted his head to the side, and his fingers tickled my skin as they brushed against it. A few seconds later, he was pulling hard on one end of the fabric before he dropped the other end from his mouth and stepped away.

"Done," he announced, watching me with the same lust in his eyes that I had in mine.

Gail walked over and looked at his work, nodding her head in approval.

"Congratulations," she said, patting him on the back. "You guys are our first winners! Go pick your gift from under the tree."

As everyone shuffled back to their seats and complained about how it wasn't fair that Jared was so good with his mouth, we made our way to the tree and studied the boxes. There were so many different shapes and sizes that I felt too overwhelmed to pick one. While Gail assured us that they were all amazing prizes, I kept envisioning something terrible like the people who get a Zonk on *Let's Make A Deal*.

The employees were wheeling in the serving trays for the buffet while we were still up there studying our options. Gail walked up and joined us, placing a hand on each of our backs.

"I know there are a lot of options, but if I can make a suggestion, I would go for those two." She nodded to two small envelopes on top of the pile of gifts. "They seem to *fit* the chemistry you guys have." She smiled and walked away, guiding the employees to form two lines at the buffet to get everyone served faster.

We grabbed the envelopes and headed back to the table. I wanted to let everyone get through the line before going up there so we weren't just standing there, waiting.

"You open yours first," Jared said, nodding to the blank white envelope in my hand.

I quickly slid my finger under the flap, opening it. I reached in and pulled out two gift cards and a piece of paper. Clearing my throat, I read it out loud.

"Enjoy a weekend getaway at the luxurious Park Springs Hotel. Two nights stay included, along with dinner and two drinks at the world-famous Range steakhouse."

Jared's brows raised in surprise, knowing how expensive this gift was. I lowered the paper and gift cards to my lap and rested my hands while I waited for him to open his. A few seconds later, his eyes widened, and he gave a nod of approval before showing me the gift card that was in his.

"Relax and melt away the holiday stress with a ninety-minute couple's massage."

"Wow," I said, impressed by both gifts.

"Sounds like a nice way to spend the weekend," he replied, his eyes locked onto mine as they tried to read what I was thinking.

"Very romantic," I commented, feeling him out.

"Might be a great way to spend New Year's Eve," he added cautiously. "If you don't already have other plans."

"You know I don't like big crowds," I whispered.

"Then would you like to be my date to a couple's massage?"

"Only if you will join me for dinner and a two-night stay in a beautiful hotel."

"It's a date," he said with a grin that spread across his face.

My stomach somersaulted as I realized that we weren't pretending this time.

Eight

Jared

My fingers drummed on the steering wheel as I waited to take the turn to Everly's house. I hated that I was heading there to drop her off and found it strange that I wasn't ready to say goodbye to her yet. After the time we'd spent together last night, followed by the fun we had at brunch, I was living on a high that I didn't want to come down from.

"Thank you again for everything this weekend," she said lightly, turning to look at me. "I can't imagine having gone through with the entire thing all on my own."

"You would have been fine," I assured her with a smile as I turned into her driveway. I put the truck in park and shifted to look at her. "But it was my honor to accompany you."

"Well, as I said before, I'm happy to repay the favor. Just let me know if there's ever anything you need my help with."

I chuckled and grinned, knowing this was my chance to get her on board.

"There is something that I need help with," I said coyly, pushing my tongue into the side of my cheek to keep from laughing.

She narrowed her eyes suspiciously and studied me.

"Alright," she said slowly. "I'm listening."

I unbuckled my seatbelt and turned to look at her, making sure I had her full attention. It wasn't that it was something overly complicated that I needed her to focus on. I simply didn't want to miss her reaction when I told her.

"Every year, the community center I grew up with puts on this holiday play. The kids dress up and rehearse for weeks—it's a huge deal. Everyone has a fun time, and we invite some of Chicago's most elite to attend. It's our biggest fundraiser of the year, and that money is put right back into the programs for the kids. Aside from funding the programs, we use some of that money to help those who need it. Things like buying groceries for a family in need or getting new shoes before school for those who can't afford them. We help a lot of families in the community, and in return, they volunteer at the community center to keep it up and running."

"That sounds amazing," she replied softly. "What do you need from me?"

I cleared my throat, forcing the chuckle back down before it slipped out.

"Mrs. Bailey always plays Old Man Grumpus—she's the best, and since her personality is naturally sour, it kinda fits her. But this year, she slipped and broke her hip, so she can't do it."

"Okay," she said, her voice more guarded than a few minutes ago.

"So, if you're up for it, I need you to be our Old Man Grumpus." I put my hands in front of me as I begged and made sure to give her the smile that usually got me what I wanted.

She pulled her head back and covered her mouth as she laughed, a snort escaping in the process.

"You want *me* to play Old Man Grumpus?" she asked, snorting again.

I nodded, too fixated on the way her dimples in her cheeks deepened as her smile stretched tighter across her face.

"I mean, I know I'm not the cheeriest person," she joked.

I laughed and leaned back against the door.

"I know that it's not as glamorous as the Christmas party, but I'm in a bind, and the show is next weekend. If you'd be willing to help me with this, I'll owe you again." I could hear the desperation in my voice and hoped she didn't pick up on it. I wanted her to help me with this because it would mean that we could spend more time together, and I really wanted that. Plus, I did need someone to fill the spot. But I didn't want her to do it out of pity or obligation. I had enough of that growing up.

She sighed and looked dramatically out of the window as she tried to keep the grin off of her face. When she turned to look at me, her blue eyes sparkled, leaving me to feel hopeful.

"Fine," she breathed as if it was the most boring thing she had ever agreed to. "I'll be your Old Man Grumpus."

I felt a quick flutter rush through me at the word *your*. I didn't know if she meant to say it, but if she did, she didn't let on.

"You have no idea how much this means," I assured her. "The kids are going to be so happy that we don't have to cancel it."

She let her smile break through as her features softened.

"Wait a minute," she said, her brow starting to furrow. "Why didn't you just do it yourself?"

"Because I'm the director," I said proudly, puffing my chest out slightly. "And the costume we have is pretty hideous..."

Nine

Everly

"Old Man Grumpus?" Becca snorted as she fell into another fit of laughter. I glared at her sitting on my bed as I pulled up my leggings and tossed my jeans to the floor. "How does he know you so well in such a short period?"

Her cheeks were flushed from laughter, and she was getting way too big of a kick out of this.

"Haha," I said sarcastically, rolling my eyes at the joke.

After I agreed to help out on Sunday, Jared and I swung by the community center to pick up the costume that I would be wearing in front of hundreds of people. Since school was still in session for a few more days, he had decided to wait to start the nightly rehearsals until tonight. The only good part so far was that Mrs. Bailey hated trying to talk into the headset that they gave her, so she always insisted that someone else narrate for her, which meant that I didn't have any lines to memorize. I just had to show up to rehearsal and go where they told me to, which was good since we only had three nights for me to practice before the show on Saturday.

"I invited you over to be helpful," I reminded her with my *mom* look.

"Oh honey, I don't think there's *any* help at this point," she laughed, holding up the tattered green fabric that was thin enough you would be able to see skin through it.

"What am I going to do?" I groaned, plopping down on the bed. "I promised that I would help him, but I don't want to go out there and make a total ass of myself on stage in front of everyone."

"It won't be that bad," she tried to assure me. "Remember when you were the ugly duckling in the school play and cried for two weeks because you thought everyone was really calling you ugly?"

I laughed softly and plopped back on the bed, remembering the play and how embarrassed I had felt back then. Becca was one of the beautiful ducks, and I had been jealous from the start. I had come home and cried to my parents, telling them that I was chosen to be the ugly duck because I was the ugliest girl in the class. They held me as I cried and then sat me down in front of a mirror to repeat positive things about myself, as they said them.

"This is different," I countered. "We're not in second grade anymore."

"No," she agreed. "We're not. But you are still beautiful, and we're going to make this the sexiest, gorgeous-looking Old Man Grumpus that Chicago has ever seen!"

She reached down and grabbed my hands, pulling me up.

"Come on, we have work to do!"

I groaned, thinking about how nice it would be to just sit on the couch and watch tv instead of whatever crazy plan she had in mind. We had both worked a half-day, calling it a hump day miracle when we were able to leave early. She had promised to help me find something to fix the costume, while I had promised to pick up her favorite Chinese food. I had fulfilled my end, and now she was ready to fulfill hers.

Two hours later, we were rushing back into my house with arms full of shopping bags. I kicked the door closed to keep the snow from blowing in with the wind that was whipping past us. I set the bags down on the couch then pulled my gloves and beanie off.

"I think they got the weather wrong on the news," Becca commented, looking out the window to the street. "That's not a light snowstorm by any means."

"Yeah," I muttered, still shivering from the bitter cold. "They said that we wouldn't get the big storm until Christmas Eve, but it looks like it started a few days early."

"What time are you supposed to meet Jared at the community center?" she asked, checking her watch.

I pulled out my phone, checking the time and if there were any new text messages from him.

"In an hour."

"Well, let's get you changed and ready to go so you're not rushing in this weather."

I felt my stomach flip-flop with dread, wondering what he would think when he saw what we did with the costume. It was too late for him to change his mind now.

Ten

Jared

I was up front, getting the kids situated as they shuffled in from the cold. Thankfully, they all knew where to go and what to do since we had been doing this for a few weeks. The unfortunate part was that they were overly hyper and excited with today being their last day of school before winter break. It was Wednesday, meaning the weekend would be here soon, as would Christmas, if you were the kind of person who looked forward to that.

I greeted the parents that were able to make it and made note of who had come with someone else's family. It wasn't uncommon for one of the kids to show up with another family since everyone in this community was good about looking out for one another. If a parent had to work one night, they asked another parent to cover for them and would help out another time. It was a beautiful dynamic that benefited the group as a whole.

It was almost six o'clock, and I knew that Everly would be showing up any minute. Or at least, I hoped that she would. It wouldn't surprise me if she changed her mind and backed out on me the second she got home and took a look at the costume that I had given her. We had needed a new one for years, but since this play only happened once a year, we didn't bother throwing any of the money that we raised toward getting a new costume. We could be feeding families instead. Our donors that attended were more interested in watching the kids perform and didn't seem bothered by the outfit that was barely held together by threads at this point.

The door opened, and a gust of wind pushed in, that sent a stack of papers flying off of the desk in the corner of the room. I brought my arm up to cover my face while I tried to catch my breath. As I lowered my arm, I saw Everly standing there, desperately trying to pull the heavy door closed so it would latch shut.

"Here, let me help you," I offered, rushing over to grab the handle. I yanked hard against the wind before it slammed into place and locked.

Her hair was blown across her face as she tried to collect herself.

"Are you alright?" I asked, reaching my hand out to help her.

"I'm good, thank you," she said breathlessly. "That wind is something. I thought I was going to blow through the door," she laughed, brushing a strand of hair out of her face.

"Well, I'm glad that you made it here safely. Sorry for dragging you out in this bad weather."

"Eh, I didn't have anything else to do." She shrugged and set her purse down on the counter before bending over to pick up the papers that had flown off.

I was about to help her when she turned to grab one, her ass swinging in my direction. Lime green leggings were clinging to her toned legs and stretched tightly across her plump globes that begged to be touched. I swallowed hard, trying to force myself to think about something else. *Anything else.*

Quickly, I bent down and picked up the remaining papers before collecting the pile from her and set them back on the counter. She smiled nervously and unzipped her jacket before pulling it off and hanging it over her arm.

I realized that I was staring at her when she raised her brows and smiled, waiting for me to guide her on where to go and what to do.

"Sorry," I said, clearing my throat. "Let me show you where you can put your stuff, and then we'll get started."

She followed me to the back and picked one of the empty lockers to leave her coat and purse. I was talking with Shirley, the director of the community center, while she got situated and hadn't heard her come up behind me. Shirley's eyes lit up as she lifted her hands to her mouth, completely ignoring whatever it was we were talking about as she looked behind me.

I turned around and felt my jaw drop as I looked at Everly. Her brown hair was pulled up and tucked into the mask she was wearing on top of her head so we could still see her face. Her body was covered head to toe in the same lime green color of her leggings, only it wasn't just leggings. It was some sort of full-body latex-looking outfit that had me thinking inappropriate thoughts about what I wanted to do to her. I had to clear my head, or it wasn't going to be my *heart* that was going to grow a few sizes.

"I still need to put this on," she said shyly, holding up the frayed fabric of the costume I had given her. "But I need help, so I don't tear it."

"Oh, honey," Shirley said quickly. "I don't think you need that at all. You look simply stunning! With the mask on and the green covering your whole body, I can't see any reason that you need to wear that old, hairy thing."

I laughed and nodded my head in agreement.

Everly's eyes shot open in surprise as she ran a hand down the smooth fabric.

"Oh, I wasn't trying to get out of wearing the other one," she admitted sheepishly. "It was just a little see-through, and I didn't want to risk lights shining in odd places and giving the donors a show they didn't pay for."

"Yeah, unfortunately, that one is pretty much on its last leg," I said with a heavy sigh. "But like Shirley said, if you're comfortable in that, I think it's perfect. The only other outfit change that you'll have is when we add the Santa suit toward the end."

She looked down self consciously and pulled her bottom lip in between her teeth before looking back up at me.

"Are you sure that it's okay? It's awfully tight."

"It's no different than what we see on tv. Besides, he's naked all the time, it's just that no one pays attention to it because he's so hairy."

"That's true," she laughed. "I just don't want to offend anyone, especially the parents or any of the kids," she whispered as a few came rushing over to us.

"Are you the new Old Man Grumpus?" Susy asked, looking up at Everly.

"I am," she replied nervously, looking from Susy back up to me.

"Wow!" Everett said, his eyes wide with surprise. "You look just like the one on tv!"

"Thank you," she giggled, her shoulders relaxing some. "I'm excited to do this play with you guys."

"I'm playing Cindy," Susy said proudly as a woman walked up behind her and placed a hand on her shoulder. I heard Everly's gasp before I saw what was happening.

"Hello, Everly," a sharp tone bit out.

I looked up and found the woman from the restaurant staring at us, eyes narrowed with her hand gripping Susy's shoulder possessively.

"This is my aunt, Staci," Susy explained, looking behind her. "My mom had to work, so she brought me, so I didn't have to ride the bus by myself."

"They know who I am," Staci said coldly.

"How do you all know each other?" Shirly asked, looking between us. I glanced at Everly, her face a shade paler than a few minutes ago.

I was about to speak but had no idea what to say; I felt completely blindsided by seeing her there. What were the chances that she would show up now? In all of the weeks that Susy's mom had to miss rehearsal before, this was the first that Staci had been sent to take care of her.

"Well, Everly used to date my boyfriend, Tom." Staci pulled

her shoulders back then turned to scowl at me. "And it seems she's moved on to *him*."

I narrowed my eyes at her, wondering what Tom saw in such a bitch of a woman. But then again, he didn't seem that smart to begin with if he left someone like Everly for someone like Staci.

"Oh," Shirley said, taken aback by the news. "I didn't know you were seeing anyone!"

Her face lit up, probably relieved to know that I wasn't some poor, pathetic man who couldn't find a woman to date me. She had been running the community center since I was a little boy and started showing up on my own when my mom was working three jobs to support us. In all of the years that she'd known me, I had never brought a woman around before.

"It's a new relationship," I muttered quietly, still glaring at Staci.

"I thought you said you guys have been together six months?" Staci questioned, releasing her grip on Susy to fold her arms across her chest.

I pinned her with a look and refused to acknowledge it.

"Well, we should get started before the weather gets too bad," I said dismissively, placing a hand on Everly's lower back to guide her out to the stage where everyone else was already waiting.

We all walked in silence as Staci's heels clicked against the floor before she stormed off to take a seat with the other parents. I tried to shift my mindset to focus on the play and get Everly up to speed. The kids were amazing with helping me, and in no time, we were doing a complete run-through of the play. Everly laughed and jumped right in, surprising me with how easily she adjusted to everything. I was worried that she would be too nervous—or worse, upset with seeing Staci, but she didn't seem bothered at all.

After we ran through everything a second time, I decided to wrap everything up for the night before the weather got too bad for everyone's drive home. The kids rushed off to put their costumes away and said goodbye to Everly on their way out. I was used to being the last one to leave and lock up for the night.

Everly was in the back, pulling her coat and purse out of the locker, when I found her.

"Thanks for being such a good sport about everything," I said as I pulled my coat on.

"It was so much fun," she smiled. "The kids are truly amazing."

"They seem to have taken a quick liking to you as well."

She blushed and turned to the side as she tucked the mask into the cubby with the old costume.

"I like the new costume, by the way," I added, letting my eyes roam over her body now that no one else was around.

"Thank you," she said quietly, tucking a strand of hair behind her ear as she turned to face me.

I stepped closer, my fingers itching to touch her.

"I was worried that it was too tight," she whispered as I

stood in front of her. I could feel her breath hot against my neck as she spoke.

"I wouldn't mind if it were a little bit tighter," I admitted, swallowing as my throat strained against the words that I shouldn't be saying.

"If it were any tighter, I would practically be naked."

Her words sparked a fire inside that I couldn't put out if I tried. A low growl escaped my lips before they crashed down on hers.

Eleven

Everly

I moaned as he kissed me, his hands eagerly moving down until his fingers were digging into my ass to lift me. My legs spread to welcome him as he held me against the lockers, our mouths working against each other in a frenzy. His hands grazed my body, touching every inch as if he couldn't get enough.

"Oh, god," I moaned, ready to rip off these leggings so I could feel him inside of me. Everything felt on fire as he touched me, and I was eager for more.

My legs wrapped tightly around his waist as he trailed kisses down my neck. I could feel the heat between my legs as his hand gently dipped down to rub me through the thick fabric.

"I need more," I panted in his ear. "Please, Jared. I want you so bad."

I heard another growl from him as he lowered me to my feet. His lips landed on mine again as he worked to get his coat off. I was thankful that I hadn't put mine on yet since it felt like I already had too many layers of clothing on. We continued kissing as we walked aimlessly, our hands roaming over each other's bodies as he stripped off pieces of clothing.

We stopped for a brief second as he lifted my shirt and pulled it up and over my head, leaving me in a white lace bra. The cold air made my skin prickle, a welcomed sensation against the heat that was coursing through it.

We were back to kissing when I felt something behind my foot, causing me to trip. Jared's hands caught me as he steered me to the side, out of the way of the light that was bolted to the floor of the stage. There was no one else in the building except for us, but the thought of having the room filled with people in the seats, watching while we had sex on the stage, sent a rush of electricity through me.

I was full on panting, clawing at his ripped muscles as if my life depended on it. I hadn't been this turned on ever. There was something about him that seemed to awaken this sexual beast that somehow had been lurking inside of me all of these years.

Skillfully, he helped me to the floor before situating himself on top of me. He caressed my cheek with his thumb as he waited for me to open my eyes and look at him.

"You're so beautiful, Everly."

"Thank you," I moaned as I reached my hand down and ran it along the length of his erection that was ready to burst against the tight fabric of his jeans.

He chuckled and nipped my ear while allowing me to rub him while my hips started grinding beneath him.

"Are you sure you want to do this?" he asked, his voice strained as my fingers desperately tried to work his zipper down.

"Yes," I growled. "I can't wait any longer. I want this, and I want it now."

He moaned as I slipped my hand inside and rubbed him through his briefs. Quickly, he pulled away and stripped himself to nothing while grabbing a condom out of his pocket. He laid it to the side while he came back and kneeled in front of me.

I lifted my hips, desperate to get my leggings off. The fabric was thicker than I remembered and was frustratingly hard to get off. My body was on the edge of coming undone, and I needed this release more than I needed my next breath.

"Just tear them," I moaned loudly.

He looked down at me and arched a brow before he hooked his fingers in the top and gently tugged them down until they were at my knees. I had enough room to spread my legs wide enough for him that I didn't care at that point. He quickly rolled the condom on before I grabbed him and eased him inside of me as I pushed my panties to the side.

I gasped as his dick slipped in, gliding effortlessly thanks to how wet I was. I arched my back and swiveled my hips, needing to feel him. He started thrusting, building up the pace as he reached up and pulled the cups of my bra down, exposing my pebbled nipples. I scratched my nails down his back and lifted my hips to meet each thrust as he lowered his head and pulled a nipple into his mouth.

He sucked hard, the sensation sending me nearly over the edge as he pounded harder inside of me. As he continued to take turns on each nipple, he dipped a finger in between us and started rubbing my clit.

I tilted my head back and moaned. Everything felt amazing as he worked every sensitive part of my body. I let my head fall to the side and opened my eyes, visioning the onlookers sitting in the chairs as they watched us. I was chewing my lip as the thoughts consumed and hadn't noticed that he was staring at me.

"Imagining us in front of a crowd?" he asked, his voice low and gruff.

I nodded, too aroused to deny it.

"Do you like being watched?"

"I don't know," I whispered, focusing on a seat in the front row. "I think so."

He turned his head where I was looking and kept fucking me harder.

"Picture a man sitting right there," he nodded. "Right in the front row. Watching as I fuck you. He's got his hard cock in his hand, stroking it as he watches your pussy coat my dick with how wet you are."

"Ahh," I cried out, feeling the tingle of an approaching orgasm.

"Or maybe I spread you out in front of your audience and tie you to a bed so you can't move. They'll all get to see you naked and waiting to be fucked. I'll show them how good your pussy tastes as I eat it. Or maybe I'll have you finger yourself so they can see what you like or how tight that little cunt is."

I pictured everything he said as I closed my eyes and felt my body tremble as the orgasm shot through me. He started slamming into me harder, each thrust sending him that much closer to the edge before he came hard and loud in my ear.

We were both sweaty and spent as he rolled off of me and laid on the cold floor next to me.

"That was fucking amazing," he said with a heavy breath.

"You're telling me," I agreed, glancing down to see my tights still stuck around my knees, leaving me fully exposed. I tried to close my legs, but my body was so deliciously sore that I couldn't move if I wanted to. I made an effort to pull my bra back up, but that was it.

"We should get going before that storm gets worse and we get stuck here." He groaned as he pushed himself up off of the floor and extended his hand to me before noticing my tights. "Ooops," he laughed, bending down to help pull them back up my legs.

I lifted my butt as he pulled the thick fabric over it, his eyes flashing with something as his hand grazed my bare skin.

"There you go," he said quietly, standing back and extending his hand to me.

I took it and pulled myself up, trying to stifle the groan that threatened to come out. Sex on the floor used to be a lot easier when I was younger.

"Thank you," I said, looking around to find my shirt.

Jared grabbed our clothes from the floor and handed it to me before he dressed quickly. I was disappointed when his beautiful body was covered again, but having felt it a few minutes ago was a nice memory to hold onto instead.

Once we gathered the rest of our stuff and got our coats on, we headed outside. I shivered and rubbed my hands together as I waited for him to lock the door. The snow had accumulated quickly while we were inside, blanketing my car in an ice cave that covered the tires.

The locks clicked in place before Jared turned around and frowned, taking in my predicament.

"Where the hell did all of this snow come from?" he grumbled, adjusting his gloves.

"I think they misjudged the storm that was coming for Christmas. It seems it decided to show up a few days early."

"Yeah, like a whole week early," he groaned, letting out a heavy breath.

"I can give you a ride home if you'd like," he offered, shaking his head at the state of my car.

"It's okay, I can try to dig it out." I shivered at the thought of standing here for an hour, trying to free my car, when I knew that I didn't have anything that would be useful. Maybe if I happened to have a *shovel* in my trunk, that would be helpful, but since I wasn't planning to bury any bodies any time soon, it wasn't something that I kept handy.

"I don't want to sound like a dick, especially a week before Christmas," he chuckled. "But you're not going to dig that out."

I gently elbowed him, pretending to be offended even though I knew that it was true.

"Fine," I sighed. "If you can give me a ride, that would be great."

I meant for it to come out sarcastically, but my voice betrayed me when it hitched on the word *ride*. While I hoped that he hadn't heard it, the mischievous smirk curling up the corners of his lips confirmed that he had.

"I would love to give you a ride." He licked his lips, pulling the bottom one in between his teeth before popping it free. "Come on, my truck is over here."

He led the way to the only other vehicle in the parking lot and pressed the button to unlock the doors. I stared in surprise for a few minutes, taking in the massive size of the tires on his truck. It wasn't huge like one of those monster trucks that you see on tv that crush other cars, but they were still a lot bigger and thicker than most trucks. Why hadn't I noticed how big and massive it was when he picked me up for the party? Maybe it was because I was so consumed with anxiety that I wouldn't have noticed if he showed up in a school bus that night.

"That's your truck?" I said, looking over at him to find a proud look on his face.

"It sure is."

"It's huge. I don't remember it being this big," I laughed nervously, feeling embarrassed that I hadn't paid attention to it before now.

His grin pulled tighter across his face as he rocked back on his heels.

I shook my head.

"I meant the truck."

"I'm sure you did," he chuckled, walking around to the passenger side to let me in.

I felt my skin flush with heat when he touched me and wondered if I would ever stop feeling this way with his touch. I tried to think back to when I was dating Tom and wondered if I had ever felt that electricity with him when we first started dating. If I did, it must have fizzled out quickly because it would have been nothing compared to this.

I sat patiently while Jared scraped the thick layer of ice off of his windshield. The heater was on, warming me to where I was nice and comfy. A few minutes later, he jumped in and closed the door, forcing a clump of snow to fall from the roof down the windshield.

"Alright, let's get out of here," he said as he put the truck in reverse and headed to my house.

I looked out the window on the drive home, taking in the beauty of the snow around us. It was so calm and peaceful outside with everyone off of the streets and cuddled up at home. When we got closer to my street, I noticed that the lights were off in almost every house we passed. My stomach knotted when I saw the giant limb that had broken, taking down the power line.

"Great," I muttered, leaning back in my seat.

Jared leaned forward to get a better look.

"That doesn't look good," he observed.

"They were supposed to send someone out to cut the tree back so it wouldn't be so close to the power line, but no one has been out yet."

"You're welcome to come stay with me," he offered, pulling into my driveway and putting the truck in park.

"Oh no," I rushed out. "I don't want to inconvenience you."

"You're not. I insist."

I felt the heat rush through me at the thought of being alone with him another night. This time we wouldn't have to worry about the awkwardness of not having sex, given what happened earlier. But still, it felt weird to take him up so easily on his offer.

"You've done a lot for me already, thank you. I'll be fine." I smiled and tried to force it to reach my eyes.

"If you don't have power, then you don't have heat. I'm not about to leave you in a cold house with no power or heat during the worst storm we've had in God knows how long."

I laughed nervously, trying to put my bravest face on.

"I promise, I'll be okay. I have plenty of warm blankets to cuddle up with and wine to keep me toasty on the inside. Besides, I'll be heading to bed soon anyway, so I won't even need the power."

He ran a hand over his face in frustration before looking at me again.

"Just go get what you need for tonight and tomorrow, and let's get going," he said, raising a brow at me to challenge him. "I don't feel like staying in a cold house with no power, and I'm not about to leave you in one either. So, if you're not willing to come with me to my house, then I have no choice but to stay at yours. Make a good choice, Everly," he teased with a wink.

"Fine," I grumbled and pulled the handle to the door. I rushed inside, wondering if sexy lingerie counted as something that I would *need* tonight. I sure hoped so.

Twelve

Jared

I tossed another log on the fire and watched with satisfaction, the embers floating in the air as it started to burn. Everly was in the bathroom getting changed, while I worked on getting the house warm. Thankfully, I still had power when we got here, and the heater had kept it nice and warm. I didn't really *need* to start a fire, but having her here made me want to.

Just like, I didn't *need* to open a bottle of wine but wanted to share it with her when she said she was going to drink a glass at home. Everything was screaming romance, but for once, it didn't freak me out. Maybe, it was because Everly didn't freak me out.

A few minutes later, I heard the door open and turned to find her wearing a baggy hoodie and another pair of tights, these ones black instead of lime green. Her hair was piled loosely on top of her head, and she looked relaxed and comfortable. It had me itching to get out of my clothes and into sweats.

"I poured you a glass of wine," I said, nodding to the coffee table where I had also set out a plate of cheese and crackers in case she was hungry.

"Thank you," she replied sweetly, smiling as she sat down on the couch and picked up the glass. She brought it to her lips and took a sip, her lips parting slightly to let the liquid in.

I swallowed hard, my dick starting to strain against my jeans.

"I'm going to go get changed, but help yourself to anything you need. I'll be back in a few minutes."

She nodded and reached forward, grabbing a cracker from the plate.

I went to my room and quickly changed, wondering if she had eaten dinner before she went to the community center. I knew I hadn't had time to and was planning to grab something on my way home. I could order a pizza, but the likelihood of anyone delivering in this weather was slim.

I joined her in the living room, relieved to see that she was enjoying the snack I had left out.

"I didn't get a chance to eat before rehearsal, so I was going to cook something real quick. Are you hungry?" I asked, hoping she would say yes so I could cook for her.

She shook her head no and covered her mouth with her hand while she finished chewing her cracker.

"I was planning to eat when I got home," she said after she swallowed her bite.

"Well, how about I make us some dinner then?"

"I can come help you cook," she offered, setting her glass down on the coffee table.

"I've got it but thank you," I said, waving my hand for her to stay sitting on the couch. "I'll bring you some more wine, though, if you'd like?"

"Sure, thank you."

I smiled and grabbed the bottle from the kitchen, refilling her glass before I got started cooking. I loved the layout of my house because it allowed me to be in the kitchen but see everything happening in the living room with its open concept. There was a breakfast bar that separated the two rooms and a small dining table off to the side of the kitchen that I never used. Usually, it was just me, and I always ate by myself on the couch.

Since I hadn't planned on having company tonight, I had no idea what to make. Hell, I couldn't even remember what I had in the fridge because my mind was so distracted from having her here. Excitement coursed through me, and I felt like a teenager again with his first crush. I wanted to do anything and everything to impress her.

Every few minutes, I found myself looking into the living room to find her on the couch, drinking her wine and eating crackers while laughing at the funny videos playing on the tv. It warmed my heart to see her so happy and to know that she felt comfortable here with me.

I cracked a few eggs into the skillet, deciding that omelets would be the quickest and easiest meal to prepare this late at night. I had already cut up some veggies and ham when she turned to look at me, smiling happily.

"That smells delicious, what are you making?"

"Omelets," I replied with a grin. "But, I should have asked if that sounded good before I started them." I laughed nervously, feeling stupid for not asking her before I just started cooking.

"I *love* eggs, and omelets happen to be my favorite."

"Is there anything that you don't like in them?"

"Nope," she shook her head. "I'm not a picky eater. I'll pretty much eat anything."

I nodded and turned my attention back to the stove, flipping the egg before I accidentally burned it. Once the food was ready, I served it and went to the living room, handing her a plate before joining her on the couch.

"My mouth is watering just looking at this," she commented, rubbing her lips together.

I looked away, trying to keep the dirty thoughts out of my head as I focused on the food on my plate. I cut into the omelet and took a bite, hoping it would silence the rumbling in my stomach before she could hear it.

She closed her eyes and let out a soft moan as she chewed. I felt my dick hardening as the sound floated around me and wished that I was the one eliciting that noise from her.

"This is delicious," she said, opening her eyes to find me straining to keep mine on the tv.

"Thank you," I replied, giving her a quick smile before turning away. I didn't need her to see the flush in my skin as my arousal pushed harder against my briefs.

Thankfully, we ate in silence after that, both of us devouring our food as if we hadn't eaten in days. I had no idea how hungry she was, so I doubled everything and made both of us giant omelets that took up the majority of the plate.

We both finished at the same time, leaning forward to set our empty plates on the coffee table. She leaned back and rested a hand on her stomach, looking completely satisfied.

"Did you get enough?" I asked, waiting to get comfortable until I knew that she didn't need more food.

"I couldn't possibly fit another bite in me," she laughed. "That was wonderful, and I am beyond full."

"Good, I'm glad."

She tilted her head to the side and studied me for a moment.

"What?" I asked softly, suddenly feeling self-conscious. "Do I have egg on my face?"

"No," she giggled. "I just can't figure out why you're still single."

I smiled and let out a laugh, relieved.

"Wait--," she paused, leaning forward, her face suddenly serious. "You *are* single, aren't you? Why didn't I ask that before?"

I laughed harder, feeling uncomfortable with my overly full stomach.

"No, I'm actually seeing someone," I said coyly, enjoying the look of panic on her face.

Her jaw dropped as her eyes bulged out.

"What?! Why didn't you tell me?"

I tried to stop myself but couldn't.

"I thought you knew." I shrugged dismissively and pretended to watch the tv.

She threw her hands up in the air and looked around wildly as if she expected some mysterious woman to appear out of thin air.

"How would I know?!"

Her voice raised another octave, and I felt bad for letting her panic.

"Well, you were there when I agreed to date you. I thought we were in on this together," I joked, turning to give her my full attention.

"You brat!" she scolded, reaching over to punch me playfully. I tried to lean forward and move out of the way, but she was too quick for me.

"You're cute when you're mad," I chuckled, watching the corners of her mouth turn up.

She rolled her eyes and folded her arms over her chest, pretending to be mad still.

"Then again, now I see why you're still single," she joked, raising a brow while pursing her lips.

"Just haven't found the right girl," I admitted, shifting on the couch.

"How is that possible?" she asked, dropping the act of being mad.

I shrugged again. There were a lot of women who I had dated over the years, but I just hadn't found the one that felt different. Something was always missing, but I couldn't put my finger on it.

"I don't know." I pulled my mouth into a sad smile.

"Maybe you're just not looking in the right places," she said, turning to look at me.

"Or maybe the right girl just hasn't found *me*," I suggested.

"Trust me, if she knew you existed, she would be destroying everything in her path to get to you."

I let my head fall back as I laughed.

"I'm serious," she said, poking me in the arm with her finger. "I have never met a man like you."

"Is that a good thing?" I joked.

"Yes, it's a very good thing. You're caring and sensitive but not in a wimpy kind of way. You carry yourself with confidence without being cocky or arrogant. You're genuine and don't pretend to be something that you're not just to impress others around you."

I listened as she spoke but couldn't see the same things she saw.

"You haven't known me long enough to know those things to be true," I admitted, feeling the sting of my words.

"Okay, so maybe I haven't known you that long," she agreed, "but I know what I've seen."

"And what's that?"

"A man who is kindhearted and caring. One who makes a woman wait to have sex to make sure that she's not rushing into something she might later regret."

I felt the blood pulse through me, my anger starting to build up as memories of my mother floated to the surface.

"That doesn't make me anything special, Everly. Every woman should be respected."

"Yeah, but so many guys would have looked the other way and gone for it. They don't care whether or not the woman regrets it later, as long as she says yes in the moment. For them, yes is a green light."

"It shouldn't be," I argued, trying to keep the anger out of my voice. "If you can tell that someone isn't fully certain of their decision, then you should always take that as a no."

I looked away at the tv.

"You're really passionate about this, aren't you?" she asked curiously.

I pulled my lips into a thin line and nodded, still refusing to look at her.

"Can I ask what happened?" Her voice was soft, her words sincere. She wasn't prying because she had heard the rumors that used to float around me when I was a kid.

I let out the ragged breath that I had been holding and turned to look at her. I hated talking about my childhood because people always did one of two things—1. Judge my mom for getting herself into a bad situation or 2. Pity me for having a mom who had to make those kinds of decisions.

"My mom was raped when she was a teenager. No one believed her and called her terrible names. She ended up pregnant with me, and her parents kicked her out of the house and disowned her. She didn't have any family or friends to turn to, so she decided to have me and do the best that she could to raise me on her own."

I watched the sadness flash across Everly's face as she listened.

"She worked three jobs to take care of me and raised me the best she could before she got sick. I spent a lot of time at the community center, and they quickly turned into the only family that we had. My mom knew that she could leave me there for a few hours while she worked and that I wouldn't get into trouble. They kept an eye on me, and she helped out whenever she could."

"That's why you help out and give back to them," she replied as if it all made sense.

I nodded.

"My mom passed when I was sixteen. I had nowhere to go and had no idea what to do. Shirley gave me a job and let me stay with her until I got things figured out. She's been like a second mother to me ever since."

"I'm so sorry," she said, reaching over to place a hand on my arm. "I can't imagine how incredible of a woman your mom was. So strong and brave."

"She was," I agreed, feeling the weight of how much I missed her. "She was given a bad hand in life but did the best that she could with it. There were times that we didn't have more than a box of cereal to eat. No milk. Just cereal. She hated it and was always so embarrassed that she couldn't give me more."

I paused for a moment and let a memory replay in my head.

"I remember when I was ten, I didn't know that my mom had just been laid off from one of her jobs, and I had spent the entire afternoon threading Cheerios onto a roll of yarn that I had found in the closet. I strung it all over the apartment and was so proud that I had decorated for Christmas. We didn't have money for gifts, let alone a tree. But we had Cheerios strung all over the living room, and to me, it looked like Christmas.

I was so proud that I waited at the door, and when she came home, I made her close her eyes before I let her in the door. I set her purse down and turned her, so she had the perfect angle to see what I had done. When I told her to look, she was definitely surprised. Then she started crying, and I couldn't figure out what I had done wrong. She explained that she had lost her job and that she wouldn't be able to buy groceries that week."

Everly gasped quietly and covered her mouth with her hand as her eyes filled with tears.

"I thought I had done a nice thing when really I had just strung up our meals as a decoration for the next few weeks." I laughed, reaching up to wipe away the wetness that lined the corner of my eye. "But she didn't let it bother her. She shook her head and wiped away the tears. With her shoulders pulled back, she walked around the room, touching each strand and admiring it as she told me how much she loved them."

"That's so sweet," Everly said, her voice raspy with sadness.

"It made dinner easy that week. I just picked a strand for each of us, and we sat on the couch and told stories as we ate our Cheerios."

She smiled, and I felt relieved that, for once, I didn't feel the shame that I had felt for so long every time I told this story.

"I'm really sorry that you had a hard childhood," Everly said quietly. "But it made you into an incredible man. Your mom would be so proud of you."

"I wish she was still here. I miss her every single day."

She wiped a tear away and tried to blink away the rest.

"That's why I *always* make sure a woman knows what she wants. That she has control over the situation and has a say in what happens. Because my mom had that ripped away from her, and no woman should ever be forced to make the decisions she had to make."

Everly nodded and took the tissue that I handed to her. She wiped her eyes and blew her nose before turning to look at me.

"Just so you know," she said sternly. "I knew what I wanted earlier, and I don't have a single regret about it. I would do it again in a heartbeat."

I smiled as I reached over and grabbed her, pulling her in to kiss her. We might have been pretending for everyone else, but damn if this didn't feel real when we were by ourselves.

94

Thirteen

Everly

By Friday, I was a walking, ticking time bomb of nerves about to explode. The show was in one day, and I was terrified that I would mess up and ruin it for everyone. Of course, it didn't help that Staci made a point of showing up to every rehearsal after finding out that I was in the show. I was surprised that she hadn't dragged Tom along with her to make fun of me.

I was shutting off my computer, ready to leave for the day, when Gail walked over to my desk.

"Hey, Everly. Do you have a few minutes?"

I smiled and pushed my keyboard back, turning to give her my full attention. She looked around at the other cubicles, making sure no one else was around before speaking.

"What's up?" I asked, feeling the anxiety I felt whenever I had an unexpected visit with human resources.

"I wanted to talk to you about the senior advisor position that just opened."

She gave me a pointed look, and I knew where she was going.

I pulled in a deep breath and let it out slowly.

"I think you should apply for it," she said softly.

I shifted uncomfortably in my seat and looked past her to Tom's office.

"I don't know if it's the best idea," I replied sheepishly, hating that I felt so insecure.

"You've worked your butt off and deserve the promotion, Everly. If anyone should be moved up to a senior advisor, it's you."

"But what about Tom?"

"What about him?"

It was my turn to give her a pointed look as I crossed my arms over my chest.

"You know that he's not going to be happy about it. And then I'll be working alongside him as a senior advisor, which means we'll be competing against each other."

"Then maybe he needs to focus on doing his job and not worry so much about you doing yours."

I let my head fall back and laughed, knowing that Tom would never stop worrying about what I was doing. It was this obsession that he had from the moment we first started dating. That was before he insisted that I be moved to his team. At the time, he hadn't told Gail that we were dating because he didn't want her to deny the transfer. The first few years worked well, and everyone looked the other way anytime anyone suggested that I would be given special treatment working for my boss. Instead, he made sure that I was denied every opportunity I applied for and kept me right where he wanted me.

"All you need to do is apply for the job and knock their socks off in the interview. I'll deal with Tom," she said, tapping her knuckles against the top of my desk before smiling and turning to leave. "I'll let them know there's another application coming in before they start doing interviews next week."

I returned her smile and leaned back in my chair, wondering what it would be like to finally have the job I had been dreaming about for years. I loved working here and had built so many relationships with my clients that I didn't dare leave after Tom and I broke up. If I got the senior advisor position, I would be able to keep my current clients as well as take on some of the larger clients with more assets.

It was almost 5:15, and I still had thirty minutes before I had to get to the community center for rehearsal. I didn't have time to worry about applying if I wanted to get there on time since the roads were still snow-packed and icy. I grabbed my bag from under my desk and headed outside, hoping that tonight would help calm my anxiety about tomorrow.

When I got there, the backstage area was already swarming with kids in their costumes. I got dressed quickly and pulled my mask on, feeling the comfort of being able to hide my face tomorrow night in front of the hundreds of people who were showing up.

"Hey," Jared said, coming up behind me and sliding his hand across my lower back.

I felt the electricity of it sizzle across my skin and smiled.

"Hi," I replied softly as I turned to face him.

"We'll get started in a few minutes. We're just waiting on Susy."

I nodded, not bothering to mention the likelihood that we were probably really waiting on Staci since she insisted on coming every night. Instead, I talked with the kids, listening to their excitement about Christmas, which was only four days away. I thought about the holiday and how I wanted to spend it with Jared, even though it felt a little weird since we weren't really dating.

When we were here for the rehearsals, we had to keep pretending, thanks to Staci. But I found that even when it was just us by ourselves, it felt real, and I worried that maybe I was the only one who was feeling it.

Finally, Susy showed up, and we were able to get started. I kept myself distracted from thoughts of Jared by focusing on the play. We went through it from start to finish three times before he called it a night. There was one final rehearsal tomorrow before the show, which made me feel a little relieved.

"Are you ready to go?" Jared asked, coming up behind me.

I pulled on my coat and tucked the mask inside the locker for tomorrow, along with the costume. The last thing that I needed was to forget part of it and scramble, trying to remember where I left it at home.

"Yeah," I said, looking past him as Staci headed our way, with Tom right behind her.

Before we could turn to leave, they were in front of us, Tom wearing the same scowl he had when he saw Jared at the Christmas party.

"Um, who do we speak to about getting tickets for the show tomorrow?" Staci asked Jared, tapping her pointy-toed heel on the floor as she folded her arms and waited.

"That would be Shirley, but she's already gone for the night," he answered. "And last I checked, the show was already close to selling out. I don't know if there are any tickets left."

"Well, we *need* tickets," Staci argued. "Tom wants to invite the rest of the department to watch Everly perform."

I groaned quietly and rolled my eyes. Jared gave me a quick look out of the corner of his eye before tilting his head and raising an eyebrow at Tom.

"Unfortunately, the show sells out fast, and once the tickets are gone, there's nothing we can do."

"Or nothing you *want* to do," she sneered.

"It's not a matter of whether I want to or not. The Fire Marshall decides how many people are allowed in, hence why we use tickets to keep track of attendees," Jared explained with a sharp tone. "I suggest buying tickets in advance next time."

He put his hand on my lower back and guided me to the front, ending the conversation.

Everyone else had already left, making it even more uncomfortable to have Staci and Tom still here. I stepped to the side so Jared could open the door when I felt someone grab my arm.

I turned and looked, finding Tom holding onto it with anger flashing in his eyes as he looked from me to Jared.

"Ow," I winced, feeling the sting as his fingers dug into my skin. I pulled away, jerking my arm hard enough to get Jared's attention without meaning to.

He frowned and immediately stepped beside me, placing a protective arm around my waist as he pulled me into him.

"We need to talk, Everly," Tom snapped, his jaw clenched.

"About what?" I asked impatiently.

"It's private." His teeth were gritted so tightly that I don't know how he got the words out.

"I'm not going anywhere private with you. Whatever you have to say to me, can be said in front of him."

"You've lost your damn mind," he sneered, shaking his head in disgust. "You don't even know this guy, and you're acting like you're in love with him. You need to wake up, Everly. He's just after one thing, and once he gets it, he'll be gone. Just wait and see."

I rubbed my temples and closed my eyes. He was the headache I hadn't been able to get rid of for the past six months since we broke up.

"Like I said, what I do is none of your business," I snapped. "Now, if you don't mind, it's time to go."

"Oh, I do mind," he snorted. "I'm not leaving until I've said what I need to say."

"I think you've said enough," Jared said, stepping in. His

fingers slid further around my waist, resting flatly on my stomach for Tom to see.

"Gail told me that she was going to talk to you about applying for the senior advisor position," Tom said, ignoring Jared and me. "I told her that I thought it was a huge mistake and that if she really cared about your well-being, she wouldn't bother."

I felt my shoulders tense and sag, feeling the weight of the control he liked to keep over me. But suddenly, Jared pulled me tighter to him and gave me a gentle squeeze. I pulled my shoulders back and looked Tom square in the eye.

"I've already applied," I lied.

Not that he needed to know that it was a lie. All he needed to know was that he couldn't control me anymore. I would make sure of it. And if I didn't get this position, I would talk to Gail and see what my options were for transferring to another department. I knew that I would have to leave my clients behind if I moved, but at this point, I knew that I needed to get away from Tom.

"You what?" he scoffed, eyes bulging.

"You heard me."

My body was trembling, but I didn't break eye contact with him. For once in my life, I felt strong enough to stand up to him, and I had Jared to thank for that.

"Well, you just screwed up your future with the company," he bit out. He stepped forward, swinging the door open without saying anything more or checking to see if Staci was behind him. She followed him out and let the door slam shut behind them.

Once it was just the two of us, I closed my eyes and took a deep breath.

"I'm so sorry about that," I apologized, looking up at Jared, who still had his hands wrapped around my waist. I shifted so we were standing face to face so I could see him better.

"You have nothing to be sorry about. He's a dick, and I'm proud of you for standing up to him."

"Thank you."

"Did you really apply for the other job?"

"No," I laughed, shaking my head. "I was on the fence about whether or not I should. But I guess that decision is final now."

"Is it not a job that you want?" he asked.

"Oh no, it's my dream job. It's a promotion that I've wanted for a few years."

"So why haven't you gone for it before?"

"Because Tom has always stood in the way. When we were together, he would tell me how I wasn't ready for it yet or that I needed to have more clients or a longer history with them. It made sense at the time, so I didn't question it. I mean, why would my own boyfriend stand in the way of something that I wanted? It wasn't until we broke up that I realized that he was holding me back because he didn't want to work against me."

"Against you?"

"He's a senior advisor. If I became one too, we would be competing for the same clients. It's a very competitive job, and the senior advisors are given quarterly bonuses based on performance. Tom beats everyone each quarter, and I think he was worried that I would threaten that. A lot of the big clients that he has are because of me. I got those leads and helped him work them."

"Wow," he sighed, shaking his head in disbelief. "I couldn't imagine not wanting the world for you."

I felt my heart skip a beat and wondered if he was starting to feel what I was.

"Thank you," I said warmly.

He smiled and hugged me tightly against his chest, planting a tender kiss on my forehead.

"Should we get going?" he asked.

"Yeah, it's supposed to snow again tonight, and I want to get home before it gets too bad."

"Okay," he said, sounding disappointed.

I tilted my head to the side and pulled my brows together.

"Everything okay?" I asked.

"Yeah, I was just hoping that maybe I could take you to dinner tonight. But I don't want to keep you from getting home."

I felt the corners of my lips tug up in a smile.

"Well," I said, leaning up to kiss him. "What if we picked something up along the way and ate at my place?"

His lips found mine again as he pressed tighter against me.

"Sounds like a date," he answered with a cheesy grin.

It was a date indeed and not a pretend one this time.

Fourteen

Jared

I hadn't planned to stay the night at Everly's house, but when I woke up to the sun shining through the thin curtains in her room, I didn't mind it at all. I was happy when she agreed to have dinner with me and even more excited when she suggested that we pick up food and eat at her place to avoid dealing with the storm that was moving in.

We spent the night cuddled up on the couch watching movies until we both fell asleep. Then, somewhere around midnight, she woke up and asked if I wanted to go lay down in her bed. I thought about being a gentleman and going home, but I was too tired to trust myself to drive in the seven inches of snow that had already fallen.

It was a great night, and we enjoyed each other's company without having sex. That was an odd fucking thing to think about because I couldn't remember the last time I had such a great time with someone without having anything intimate involved. That sounded pretty superficial, but it was the truth.

"Good morning," she said, rolling over to smile at me. Her hair was still pulled up on her head, a little messier than it was last night. She looked gorgeous without makeup as the sun warmed her face.

"*Great* morning," I replied, brushing her cheek with my thumb. "Thank you for letting me stay over last night."

"Of course, you're always welcome here."

We both laid there lazily, neither of us bothering to get out of bed. I reached over and picked up my phone to check the time. It was just after eight, and I already had a few text messages from Shirley about some crazy woman who had found her phone number and called demanding tickets to the play tonight.

I rolled my eyes and set my phone down, knowing that I would have to deal with the Staci problem this morning before it got out of hand. But for now, I wanted to pretend it didn't exist and enjoy my time with Everly.

"Are you hungry?" I asked, turning back on my side to look at her.

She rolled over and smiled at me, something hidden behind it.

"I am," she said seductively. "And you're just what I want for breakfast."

My eyebrows shot up as my dick stirred against my boxer briefs.

"I was thinking that *you* looked like something *I* might want to eat for breakfast," I replied, scooting over and wrapping my arm around her waist to pull her closer to me.

"Is that so?" she purred against my ear as I nuzzled my head in her neck, trailing my tongue over her skin, leaving goosebumps behind.

"Mmhmm," I murmured. "I can't wait to taste you."

She moaned as my hand slipped around to the front and dipped into her panties. Her legs opened slowly, allowing me access as my finger glided across her slit. She was already wet, and I felt my dick press harder against my briefs.

I wanted to go slow and take my time devouring every inch of her body, but I couldn't wait. My dick was getting harder by the minute, my balls aching for a release. I moved down her body, licking my way across her sensitive skin until I was between her legs. She rolled onto her back and spread them further with my shoulders as I lined my mouth up to her opening.

I looked up at her one last time before I leaned forward and ran my tongue along her slit. She gasped at the contact, her fingers digging into the sheets. I licked her over and over, lazily drawing my tongue through her folds as her legs shook beside me. Tasting her was even better than I thought it would be, but the way her body reacted so easily to me was an even bigger turn-on.

She moaned quietly as my tongue worked its magic on her body. I sucked her clit a few times before replacing my tongue with my finger, giving her the pressure she needed as I worked it in small circles while my tongue dipped inside her again.

I could feel her hips bucking off of the bed as I rubbed harder, increasing the pressure the faster I went. She was on the edge and ready to come. Her breaths quickened as she gripped the sheets again, her fingers digging into the fabric as she climaxed hard. I continued to rub her, loving the way her pussy spasmed around my finger as she orgasmed.

Her legs fell limp, and her body relaxed as I pulled my hand away. I sat up and stared at her, amazed by the beautiful woman in front of me.

"You taste delicious," I said, licking my lips. "Just like I thought you would."

"Well, now it's my turn to have breakfast," she teased, sitting up and getting on her knees. She reached up and fixed her ponytail, tightening it, so her hair was out of her face. "Stand up and strip down," she commanded.

I pulled my bottom lip in between my teeth and stood up. Hooking my thumb in the top of my boxer briefs, I slowly pulled them down, letting my erection spring free. She watched intensely, her eyes widening when she saw it. Without saying a word, she called me over to her with her finger.

I stood in front of the bed and grabbed the back collar of my t-shirt, pulling it up and over my head. I was fully naked as her hungry eyes watched me.

Slowly, she reached over and grabbed my dick, wrapping her hand tightly around it. She leaned forward, locking eyes with me as she brought her mouth to me and licked the tip. I wanted to close my eyes and savor the moment, but the way she was looking at me as she slid my cock deep into her mouth was too good to miss.

Her head bobbed back and forth as she sucked me. Her fingers gripped the length that didn't fit in her mouth, sliding up and down in the same motion as her mouth. I felt myself getting closer, desperate to release.

"Everly," I moaned. "I'm so close."

She moved faster, hollowing out her cheeks as she took me further into the back of her throat. I held her head as she let me fuck her mouth.

"I'm gonna come, now," I panted, trying to give her as much warning as I could. Instead of pulling away, she wrapped her mouth tighter around my dick and kept the pace. I closed my eyes and let my head fall back as ropes of cum shot down the back of her throat. I grunted as she continued to suck every last drop out of me.

When I was done, she pulled back and planted a quick kiss on the tip before rolling back onto the bed.

My body was relaxed as I collapsed on the bed beside her.

"Out of all of the things that I'm most thankful for this year," I said lazily, laying on my back. "I'm really glad I was at the restaurant that night."

"Why's that?" she asked with a giggle, rolling onto her side to look at me.

"Because I don't want to think about how it could have been another man who got that blow job."

She let her head fall back as she laughed.

"Well, given that I was getting stood up left and right, I don't think this is something we would have had to worry about."

"None of those losers were worthy of having a chance with you, Everly."

"I'm glad it was you that night, too," she said, something in her voice changing. I rolled onto my side and studied her. "You saved me from a lot of embarrassment. If I would have gone to that party alone, I would never have heard the end of it."

"You don't give yourself enough credit. You're strong, Everly. Look at how you stood up to him yesterday. I'm proud of you for doing that."

"That was because you were there with me. If it were just me by myself, I wouldn't have done that. I wouldn't have had the guts to."

I hated the feeling that was knotting in my stomach, knowing that she was telling the truth. I had noticed how she seemed afraid of him and cowered before she stood up for herself.

"I can't believe that he wanted to invite the entire department to the play tonight," she continued with a sigh. "It's like he gets off on embarrassing me. I'll always be stuck under his thumb if he has any say in it."

"Then don't give him a say," I blurted out.

"It's not that easy," she laughed. "I was with him for five years. If anything, I let him mold me into this pathetic person that I am today. Someone who worries more about his happiness than my own."

"I can understand that," I said gently, trying to keep my personal feelings at bay. "My mother was like that."

"What do you mean?" she asked.

"After she was raped, she stayed working for the bastard. He had convinced her that she owed it to him and that it was her fault because she dressed too provocatively at work. He said that she had asked for it, and when she told him she was pregnant, he told her that she would need to work more hours to afford her maternity leave if she wanted to take any when she had the baby."

"Did she know him well?"

"He was her boss. She worked for him for several years before it happened. He made her believe that she couldn't make it on her own, and that fear kept her right where he wanted her. Finally, she decided that she had enough and quit."

"Wow," Everly breathed. "Good for her, but it sucks that she had to go through all of that. I'm so sorry."

I shrugged and let out a heavy breath.

"It happens more often than people talk about. Women are put in these situations all the time, and most of them don't see they're being used and manipulated until it's too late."

I turned to look at her, hoping that she would pick up on what I was trying to say.

"Like me with Tom." She rolled onto her back and stared at the ceiling. The fun and relaxing morning that we started with turned sour quickly.

After breakfast, I took a few minutes to call Shirley while Everly took a shower. I would have offered to take one with her, but she didn't seem interested in having me touch her after our discussion earlier. I didn't blame her, but I also hated that we even had to talk about it to begin with. It felt like I was living my mom's nightmare all over again by watching Everly struggle to gain control over her life with Tom. It wasn't the exact same situation, but I could see the power that he held over her.

By two o'clock, we headed over to the community center to run through a few rounds of rehearsals before the show started at seven. Everly and I didn't speak to each other much while we were there, and it seemed like everyone noticed. I excused myself to handle things up front while everyone got ready. Really I just wanted to give her some space so she could relax before the show started.

I was up front at the ticket booth with Shirley when I saw Staci and Tom show up. I rolled my eyes and turned my head, letting her know I would handle them before they got to the window. She patted my hand and smiled, familiar enough with what was going on to let me deal with it.

"Hi!" Staci said with fake enthusiasm. "Should we go on in?"

I narrowed my eyes and arched a brow.

"Only ticket holders are allowed in tonight," I explained, a little more aggression in my voice than necessary.

"Oh," her face fell. "Well, then can we get two tickets?"

I shook my head and pulled my lips into a thin line.

"Sorry, the play is sold out."

"You've got to be kidding," she griped. "My *niece* is performing, and I came to see her."

"Well, unfortunately, you'll need a ticket, and we're sold out."

She stomped her foot and crossed her arms over her chest as she clenched her jaw. She looked at Tom and nodded in my direction.

"Just give us a ticket," he demanded, irritation thick in his voice.

"No."

"Excuse me?" he bit out.

"What part of *there are no tickets left* do you two not understand?" I asked, looking between the two of them.

"You're just saying no because you're trying to protect Everly," Staci muttered.

"Protect her from what?" I asked sternly, causing Shirley to flinch beside me. "From you bullying her and making fun of her? Or from you trying to bully her into doing what you want? If that's what you're worried about, rest assured that I will *always* protect her. Not only that, but I will teach her how to stand up for herself, so she never has to bother with you again. But regarding the show, WE. ARE. OUT. OF. TICKETS." My voice boomed in the small booth, causing others nearby to turn and look at us. "If you can't understand the basic concept of what I'm saying, then that's your problem, not mine."

Staci's jaw dropped open as Tom's clenched tighter. Before they could say anything more, I leaned to look past them, calling up the next person to check-in. They moved out of the way, and I watched as they walked off. Tom's fists were balled as Staci tried to hold his hand before he jerked away from her.

Once everyone was seated, and the doors were closed, I took my place backstage and sat on the stool to watch as Shirley thanked everyone for coming. Soon the play had started, and I found myself in awe as I watched Everly move around on the stage, interacting with kids as if she had been doing this for years. She was such a natural that I wondered what she would be like someday as a mother.

When the show was over, everyone piled out of the community center and headed over to the dinner that Shirley was putting on for the kids and their families. It was always something simple that the families helped out with. Tonight it was a spaghetti dinner, and I thought about asking Everly if she wanted to go.

The kids had all left, and she was finishing changing while I waited in the lobby for her. She came out a few minutes later, wearing a pair of skinny jeans tucked into some boots and a cream-colored sweater that stretched tight against her chest. It wasn't what she had on earlier, and I wondered if she had plans.

"Are you ready to go?" I asked, unsure of what to say.

"Yeah," she said, reaching into her pocket for her car keys.

"They're having a spaghetti dinner for the kids and their families tonight. Did you want to go?"

She paused for a moment, guilt flashing across her face.

"I'm sorry, I can't," she said quietly.

"Do you have plans?"

She nodded without saying anything else.

"Is it a date?" I asked, feeling my stomach tighten anxiously. While we had been spending a lot of time together—and sleeping together—we hadn't stopped to label whatever this was between us. Which meant that I didn't know that I had any right to be upset with her if she said yet.

"I wouldn't call it that," she replied nervously, fidgeting with her keys.

"Then what would you call it?"

She lowered her eyes and looked at the floor.

"Look," I said with a sigh. "I know that we haven't talked about whatever this is between us, but if we need to label it to keep you from going, then fine. I like you, Everly. A lot. And if you want me to call you my girlfriend, then that's what you are, my girlfriend. But please, don't go on this date."

"It's not that easy," she countered, tilting her head in frustration.

"Why not?"

"Because it's someone that my mom set me up with."

I narrowed my eyes and read between the lines as she looked away, avoiding eye contact.

"Who?"

"Brad."

The laughter rushed out of me before I could stop it. My eyebrows nearly shot off of my forehead as I processed what she was saying.

"You're going on a date with Brad? The guy your mom tried to set you up with and stood you up the night we met? *That* Brad?"

She nodded and looked away.

"Can't you just say no? Say that you're busy?" I offered.

"I can't do that."

"Why not?" I felt like I was on repeat at this point, not understanding why she was agreeing to do this.

"Because you don't know my mother. It's easier just to go."

I pulled my head back in surprise and looked at her. Suddenly, it felt as if I didn't know the woman standing in front of me. The girl who was so playful and confident when we were by ourselves was replaced with the timid, insecure girl I met that first night.

"Well, you know best." I kept my mouth shut after that, refusing to say any more.

"I'm not trying to upset you," she said softly.

"What does it matter? We were just pretending anyway, right," I bit out, letting my anger get the best of me.

I turned and walked out, leaving Shirley to lock up after Everly left.

Fifteen

Everly

"What's up, Buttercup?" Becca said as she walked through my front door. She stepped to the side and took in my messy bun and sweats before narrowing her eyes. "What's wrong?"

"Nothing," I sighed, pushing the door closed behind her and moping into the living room. I plopped down on the couch and pulled the blanket up to my chin.

"You're lying," she said, sitting in the chair beside me. "Do you need ice cream or Chinese food?"

"Neither," I muttered, pretending to watch tv.

She reached over and picked up the remote, turning it off.

"I was watching that," I lied, not bothering to look away from the blank screen.

"Sure you were."

"I was."

"Okay, let's get it over with. Do I need a baseball bat or a sharp pair of scissors?" she asked, leaning forward and resting her elbows on her knees.

"For what?" I turned my head and looked at her, confused.

"It's obvious that someone hurt you. So it's either Tom or Jared. If it's Jared, then I'm going to take a baseball bat and beat him until he comes to his senses. If it's Tom, then you don't need to know what I'm going to do with the scissors." She paused for a moment before adding, "never mind, it's actually better that you *don't know*. You know, for court purposes and stuff."

"It's neither of them," I muttered, turning to look away again. "I was the idiot this time."

"What did you do?"

I waited for a moment before I answered. When I saw the look on Jared's face last night, I knew that I had made the wrong decision.

"Well," she prodded.

I sighed and pushed myself up to a sitting position on the couch.

"I went on a date last night."

"With who?"

"Brad."

She leaned back in her chair and folded her legs under her as she got comfortable.

"*Brad?*"

"Brad," I confirmed.

"As in…."

"The guy who my mom tried to set me up with the night I met Jared."

"The one who—"

"Stood me up? Yup, that's the one," I said bitterly.

"Okay, so why did you go on a date with him last night?"

That was the question that I had been asking myself over and over from the moment that I left the restaurant last night.

"I didn't feel like I had a choice." I shook my head, the disappointment still weighing heavily on my shoulders.

"Why didn't you have a choice?"

"Because my mom called and told me that she had talked to him personally and informed me that I was going to meet him at Le Blue last night."

"Oh," she sighed. She knew my mother long enough to understand what I was saying without me needing to elaborate further.

A few minutes passed before either of us spoke.

"So, was the date bad?" she asked, trying to figure out why I was so depressed.

"It was just as I had expected. He was boring and talked about himself the entire time. When it came time for them to bring the check, he mentioned how my mother had bragged about how independent I was and that I didn't need a man to pay for things for me."

"So you paid for your own meal?"

"And his."

Her jaw dropped open.

"No!" she gasped. "Everly, why did you do that?"

"Because I'm a stupid, pathetic girl who likes to get screwed over?"

She rolled her eyes and waited for me to continue.

"The waitress didn't know to split the check. He had slid his hand over to my knee, and I knew where he was going with it. I told him that I wasn't feeling well and needed to leave. I was over the date and didn't want to be stuck there with him longer than necessary, so it was easier just to give her my card and have her run the whole thing."

"Wow," Becca laughed. "I don't think I've ever had a date *that* bad before. Did he at least give you a reason for why he stood you up last time?"

"Start going out with me. I'm a magnet for them," I sighed. "And no, he simply *forgot*."

We rolled our eyes at the same time.

"That's not true, and he's an idiot," she said, her tone turning more serious. "You've had great dates with Jared."

I laughed and snorted, not bothering to cover my mouth as I let my head fall back.

"Yeah, I'm really good at pretend dating but can't do the real thing to save my life." I could feel the sadness radiate through me when I thought about how happy I had been when I was with Jared. I wished that it was real because pretending had started to feel so easy. Shouldn't it have been harder if there wasn't anything between us?

"What happened with Jared?" she asked softly.

"Nothing," I shrugged. "We were just pretending."

"But were you?"

I looked at her and felt like my heart was on display. She knew me well enough to see through any excuses that I tried to give her.

"It doesn't matter," I sighed. "He didn't take it well last night when he found out I was going out with Brad."

"What did he say?"

I closed my eyes and tried to remember word for word what he had said. For whatever reason, my brain had shut down and kept it hidden. Maybe it was a defense mechanism to keep me from feeling more heartbroken, or maybe I was just finally sinking to a new level of breakdown where I couldn't process words. Who knew at this point?

"He was upset. Said something about being my boyfriend if I needed to label it."

Her face changed from surprise to sadness as she heard the hurt in my voice.

"He asked me not to go."

She slumped back into her chair, feeling the weight of the depression that surrounded me.

"But you did anyway."

"I did."

"So, what are you going to do now?" she asked, a hint of optimism in her voice.

"What is there to do? He stormed out and left. I haven't heard from him since."

"Have you tried calling him?"

I arched a brow and pulled my lips into a thin line.

"Right," she said. "What a silly thing for me to ask."

"What's that supposed to mean?" I asked, suddenly feeling defensive.

"Nothing," she said, getting up out of her chair. "Just that you are too scared of something good happening to you that you refuse to make an effort to go after it."

My jaw dropped open in disbelief.

"I'm not scared," I countered. "He walked out on *me*."

"Because you basically told him that he wasn't good enough for you to cancel the date. He wasn't good enough for you to say no to your mom. Everly, you had a great thing going. A man who genuinely cared about you and asked you to be his girlfriend. He made it clear how he felt about you when he thought you were going on the date because you didn't know where you stood with him. He's told you that he's interested in being with you, and you're sitting here like you're the victim."

I shook my head and turned away. She was right, and I hated it.

"I'm going to go so I can finish my Christmas shopping," she said dismissively. "Try not to wallow in self-pity for too long. Fix it before it's too late."

She gave me a pointed look before grabbing her purse and walking out the door.

I laid back down on the couch, thinking about what she said. As I was about to turn on the tv, I heard my phone vibrate. My stomach fluttered as I hoped that it was Jared texting me. Instead, it was Susan, asking if I could help her with a problem she was having with a client.

I didn't have the file with me and knew that I wouldn't be able to focus on anything productive, so I texted her back and let her know that I was heading into the office and would work on what she needed. It wasn't the first time that I had gone to work on a Sunday. At least no one else would be there to bother me while I worked.

Sixteen

Jared

I stared at my phone and deleted the seventh text that I had started writing to Everly. I hadn't talked to her since I walked out on her last night, and I felt anxious about it ever since. I was pissed when she told me that she was going on a date with the guy that had initially stood her up, but then I had to keep reminding myself that I didn't have any right to be mad.

The day was dragging on at an incredibly slow pace, and I knew that I wasn't going to be able to relax until after I cleared the air with Everly. I needed to talk to her but didn't know whether she wanted to speak to me. Last night, I asked her to be my girlfriend, and she still decided to go out with another guy.

My head was a mess wondering whether she had been into things as much as I was or if she had really just been pretending. It wasn't like we had been dating long enough to have deep feelings for each other, but I knew that there was more to this than just a little crush.

I sucked in a breath and held it as I typed a quick text, asking her what her plans were for the day. I pressed send and let it out, wondering whether she would bother to reply.

I set my phone down and tried to force myself to walk away and not obsess about it. There were plenty of things that I should be doing, but none of them were high on my priorities right now. Talking to Everly overrode everything, including the basics like feeding myself as my stomach growled in protest.

A few minutes later, I heard my phone chime and ran over to check it like the desperate loser I was.

Everly: I'm at work. Not sure how long I'll be here.

It was quick and kind of cold, but I tried not to read too much into it.

Me: Anything I can help with?

I smacked my palm against my forehead after I pressed send. What in the world would I possibly help with? I knew nothing about investments or what she did with them.

Everly: No, but thank you.

I sucked in a deep breath and held it. At this rate, I would pass out from holding my breath so much, but I didn't care.

Me: Okay. Let me know if you need anything.

I set my phone down and pushed it across the table to keep from typing anything else. I sounded desperate and pathetic enough already as it was.

Forcing myself to focus on anything other than her, I left my phone where it was and went to start a load of laundry. There was plenty of house cleaning that I could get done to kill some time.

Thirty minutes later, I was sitting on the couch, folding a load of towels that I had forgotten in the dryer. They weren't soft and fluffy like they were when they first came out of the dryer, but I didn't have the energy to worry about that. It wasn't like Everly was rushing right over to come take a shower and let me wrap her in my warm towels.

I shook my head and tried to clear any thoughts of her, but it didn't work. She was on my mind constantly, and I hated that I couldn't think about anything else. I finished folding the towels and put them away. The other load of laundry wouldn't be ready for twenty minutes, and then I would still have to wait for it to dry.

I gathered the trash in the house, collecting it in one bag before running it out to the trash can. The snow was falling hard again, and the news had predicted that we would get another two inches before dusk. I hated the thought of Everly driving in this weather, but it wasn't like we were on the best of terms right now. Then again, I cared more about her safety than I did this stupid *fight* we were having. I wasn't even sure if that's what you could call it since we weren't dating.

Convincing myself that I was doing the right thing, I grabbed my keys off of the coffee table and slid my coat on before rushing out to my truck. Then, without giving myself the chance to talk myself out of it, I headed to her work, wondering if I should tell her that I was coming.

Fifteen minutes later, I was pulling into the parking lot, relieved when I saw her car was still there. There were a few other cars parked a few spaces over, so I took the open space right beside her.

I pulled out my phone, ready to text her to let her know I was there when a woman came walking out of the door.

"Hey, you're Jared, right?" she said, smiling and holding the door open. "I'm Susan, Everly's friend from the Christmas party."

"Oh, hey," I said, smiling as I remembered how Everly had spoken so kindly about her. "It's great to see you again."

"You too. Are you here to see her?"

"Yeah, I was worried about her driving in this weather, so I came to give her a ride home."

"Well, aren't you the sweetest," she said, clutching her hand to her chest. "She's the luckiest girl in the world to have such a caring boyfriend."

"Thank you," I said shyly, feeling guilty for accepting her compliment.

"Well, she's up on the fourth floor. You'll see her desk in the middle cubicle." She stepped to the side and held the door for me.

"Thanks, I appreciate it," I said as I moved inside.

"Have a Merry Christmas," she called over her shoulder as she walked to the parking lot.

"You too," I hollered back, hoping she had heard me.

I let the door close behind me as I made my way over to the elevator and waited. Finally, the doors opened, and I climbed in, pushing the number four repeatedly until the doors closed and it started to move. I was equally anxious and excited to see her.

Once the doors started to open, I slid through and pushed my way out, scanning the floor for her. There was a light on at a desk in the middle where Susan said she would be, but I didn't see her. So I walked around, looking in the empty offices when suddenly something caught my eye.

In the corner office, the light was on, and voices were floating through the air. I made my way over and stopped short when I saw Everly pinned against the wall with Tom on top of her.

"Tell me you want it," he said, loud enough for me to hear through the rush of blood pulsing through my ears. "Come on, Everly, tell me how bad you want this."

I couldn't hear what she was saying, but it didn't sound the same as when she was begging me to touch her. There was something in her voice that sounded off. I kept walking until I was right outside the door, staring at them.

He pressed his body against hers, holding her in place as one hand caressed her breast. She flinched at his touch, and I watched her body stiffen.

"Stop it," she said sternly but not loud enough to get his attention.

Everything around me turned red as my anger ignited quicker than a match. Within seconds, I was on him, grabbing him by the shirt and flinging him off of her.

He stumbled back, shocked as he tried to focus on what had just happened. Then, before he could fully register who I was, I pulled my arm back and swung as hard as I could, feeling the crack of his nose against my hand.

"You son of a bitch," he yelled, reaching up to touch it.

I swung again, this time hitting him in the jaw. I could feel the adrenaline coursing through me as I tried to swing again, this time, my arm was held back by Everly.

"Jared! Stop it!" she screamed. "It's not what it looks like!"

Her words stopped me in my tracks. I lowered my arm and turned to look at her. Her face was red and flushed as she reached down and adjusted her shirt.

"What exactly do you think it looks like?" I asked. "Because to me, it looks like you were saying no, and he wasn't listening."

"You don't know what the fuck you're talking about," Tom hissed, grabbing a tissue out of the box on his desk.

"I think you should go," Everly said, looking at me.

"You want me to go?"

She nodded her head and wrapped her arms around her body.

"I think it's for the best."

I shook my head and let out an exasperated breath.

"Fine. If that's what you want."

I turned and walked away, my hand starting to ache from hitting that asshole's face.

Seventeen

Everly

I was an idiot. A big, giant, stupid idiot.

After Jared left, I immediately regretted asking him to do so. I had no idea why he was there in the first place, but the last thing that I wanted was for him to stick around and have another go-round with Tom. Not because I thought that he couldn't handle Tom, but because I worried that Tom would be his typical self and press charges against him after he got his ass kicked.

"You better tell your boyfriend that he's not welcome in this office again. If I see him, I'm going to—"

"You're going to what?" I interrupted, feeling my anger bubble over. I stood in front of Tom with my hands on my hips.

"I'll get a restraining order against him," he said, jutting his jaw out.

"Why? Because you're afraid that he'll come back and finish what he started?"

I don't know if it was because Jared had been there and left some sort of magic in the air that gave me the confidence to stand up to him or what, but suddenly I felt strong enough to stand up to him.

"I could take him," he scoffed, wiping at the blood that was still dripping from his nose.

I rolled my eyes and stepped back with my arms folded across my chest.

"You couldn't take him if you tried," I corrected. "And you're not going to get a restraining order against him. In fact, if I were you, I would start looking into other job options because I will be filing a sexual harassment report with Gail as soon as I get home."

"Sexual harassment, please." He snorted and sat down in his chair, applying more pressure to try to stop the bleeding.

"Do not dismiss this as if it didn't happen," I said angrily, placing my hands on his desk and staring down at him from the other side. "You pinned me against the wall and touched me inappropriately when I told you to stop."

"You wanted it."

"You wouldn't know what I wanted if it was staring you in the face. You're too selfish to think about anyone else. But I can promise you this—that will be the *last* time that you touch me."

I pushed away from the desk and glared at him, finally seeing him for the asshole that he was.

"I'll make sure Gail gives you a copy of the report once she has it. I've also requested to be transferred from this department if I don't get the promotion."

I watched as his face reddened with anger as I turned and walked away. I didn't bother finishing the project that we were working on. He could figure out how to fix his own damn errors. I grabbed my stuff from my cubicle and stormed out, making sure he didn't follow me.

Once I was in the car, I locked the doors and pulled out my cell phone. The snow had gotten worse since I got here, and I knew that the drive home would be difficult. I found Gail's number and pressed send, knowing that if I didn't call her now that I would talk myself out of doing it later.

I turned on the speakerphone and set my phone in the cup holder, waiting for her to answer as I got the hell out of there.

A few rings later, her voicemail picked up instead. I waited for the beep and gripped the steering wheel, hoping that it would brace me for what I was about to do.

Once I heard the end of her greeting, I began speaking.

"Hi, Gail. This is Everly. I needed to talk to you regarding an incident that just happened while I was in the office with Tom. I'll give you the details in this message and then email you a written statement as soon as I get home." I paused and took a deep breath, hoping that it didn't cut me off. Then, keeping it as short and to the point as possible, I continued.

"I went into the office today to help Susan after she sent me a message about needing help with a client. I didn't expect her to meet me there, but she showed up anyway. A little while later, Tom came in as well. Susan and I finished what we needed to, and then she left. I was heading out right behind her when Tom asked for my help. I told her to go ahead and go home, so she wasn't stuck driving in the weather. When I went to Tom's office, he mentioned that he needed help with a problem that he was having. When I asked what it was, he walked across the room and pinned me against the wall. I wasn't able to move from the weight of his body against mine. I told him repeatedly to get off of me, but he didn't listen. He continued to try to kiss me and groped my breasts before my boyfriend, Jared, showed up and pulled him off of me. I confronted Tom and let him know that I would be filing a report, however, I wanted to make sure that I told you about it as soon as possible. I'll be available on my cell phone if you get this and want to talk. Bye."

I stopped at the red light and picked up my phone, ending the call. My fingers were shaking, and I couldn't believe that I had done that.

I knew that I needed to talk to Jared and explain what happened, but as a gust of snow blew past me, I realized that I was better off getting home first. I could always call him once I got there safely.

Twenty minutes later, I pulled into my driveway and climbed out of the car, struggling to open the door against the snow that had piled up in the driveway. I carefully made my way inside, making sure to avoid moving too fast and slipping on the ice beneath me. Once inside, I kicked off my boots and rushed over to turn up the heater.

It was warm in the house but not warm enough to thaw the icy cold chill that continued to run through me. I changed into a pair of fleece pajama pants and pulled on my favorite hoodie, hoping that would help. What I really wanted was to cuddle up next to Jared and let him warm me up with his skillful hands.

I sat on the couch and turned on the TV as I got situated. My phone showed a missed call from Gail with a voicemail but nothing from Jared. I listened to her message, checking to make sure I was alright. She promised that she would get the report started immediately and have me transferred to another department first thing on Monday morning. I didn't have any idea what that meant as far as my clients, but I was too tired to care.

I was disappointed that Jared hadn't called or texted me, but then again, I couldn't blame him. I had been terrible with him the last few times we had seen each other. So, why would he want to talk to me? I knew that I needed to fix whatever this was between us, but I didn't know how.

Working off some of the adrenaline that was still in my system, I picked up my phone and dialed his number. The phone rang several times before he finally answered.

"Hello."

I closed my eyes and pulled my lips together. He was still pissed.

"Hey," I said softly, hoping to ease the tension.

Silence.

"About earlier," I started, "I'm sorry about what happened."

"Sorry that you got caught?"

I whipped my head back as if I had just been slapped.

"Caught?" I asked in disbelief. "I wasn't doing anything."

"Then why are you apologizing if you didn't do anything?"

"Because I felt bad for asking you to leave."

He huffed out an irritated breath, and I started to worry that this was a mistake. Maybe I should have given him more time to cool off.

"I don't think I can do this, Everly," he said evenly.

"Do what?"

I could feel the panic rising inside of me.

"Whatever this is between us. *Was*."

My heart started racing, thudding loudly in my chest.

"Jared, I said that I was sorry," I stammered.

"And I've told you that you shouldn't say sorry if you didn't do anything."

"So then, what are you upset about? We can try to fix it," I pleaded.

He paused for a moment, keeping me on pins and needles.

"I can't be with someone who doesn't value themselves, Everly. It's too exhausting."

I closed my eyes and pinched the bridge of my nose to keep from crying.

"It was fun while it lasted, but maybe it's for the better that we end it before things get too complicated."

"Jared," I whispered. "I know that you're upset, but can't we talk about this?"

"Talk about what? I told you that I was falling for you, and you still went on a date with a guy who stood you up. Then I walked in on your ex assaulting you, and you acted like I was the bad guy for protecting you. I can't win with you, Everly. And honestly, it's too hard trying."

"So, what are you saying?" I asked, my lip trembling.

"I'm saying that it was fun while it lasted, but I think it's best if we move on and go our separate ways."

The tears fell down my face as I cried, the line going dead a few seconds later.

Eighteen

Jared

"So, what did you get her?" Shirley asked excitedly as we shoved the bins with the costumes from the play back into the storage area behind the stage.

"Get who?" I asked, unsure of what she was talking about. I lifted another box and slid it on top of the others.

"Everly," she laughed. "It's Christmas Eve, you better have gotten her present, or you're going to have a heck of a time finding one now."

I swallowed hard before I climbed down and turned to face her.

"We're not together anymore," I said sternly before walking past her to get the other boxes.

"What?" she gasped. "Why not? You guys were the perfect couple."

"I seriously doubt that," I laughed. "It was all just a show."

"What do you mean?"

I stopped moving the boxes and wiped my hands on the

front of my jeans. I had her full attention, which meant she wasn't going to let this go.

"Everly and I weren't ever really dating. It was all fake from the start."

"Fake?" she repeated, still not buying it.

I nodded.

"I was picking up dinner a few weeks ago and overheard a conversation that she was having with her ex. He was giving her a hell of a time about being stood up, so I decided to swoop in and pretend to be her boyfriend. She needed a date to her work's Christmas party, so I offered to go. Unfortunately, her boss is the same jerk that I met that night. After the party, I asked her to help out with the play. When she ran into Staci, we had to keep the act up since she was dating Everly's ex-boyfriend."

"But you guys get along so well. So why didn't you try to date?"

"I wanted to," I laughed, sitting on one of the sturdier boxes. "But she didn't want to."

"She said that?"

"In not so many words."

Shirley narrowed her eyes and frowned.

"Nope," she said firmly. "There's more to that story. Spill it."

"There's nothing to spill. She went on a date with another guy on Saturday, and I caught her making out with her ex at work on Sunday."

"What?!" She covered her mouth with her hand. "Did you ask her about it?"

"Yeah, and she told me that she had to go on the date because her mom had set it up. Not only did her mom *force* her to go, but it was also with the same guy who had stood her up the night that I met her."

"And what about her making out with her ex?"

"Well, I guess they weren't technically *making out*," I said bitterly. "I caught him pushing her up against the wall in his office. It sounded like she was saying no. He didn't listen."

Her face fell, and I knew that she could predict where this was going.

"What did you do?"

"I pulled him off of her and then hit him a few times."

She covered her face with her hands and muttered my name a few times.

"What did she do?"

"She freaked out and made me leave."

"Have you talked to her since then?"

I rolled my head back and forth on my neck, trying to relieve some of the tension that was building with this conversation.

"She called me yesterday."

"And?"

"I told her that I thought that whatever this was between us should be over."

"Why?"

I sighed and blew out a frustrated breath as I leaned forward and rested my elbows on my knees.

"Because it's too hard. She refuses to value herself enough to say no to people and then gets mad when I try to stick up for her."

"Has she told you anything about her mom?"

"Only that she's tough on her. Everly has tried to get her approval all of her life, but nothing is ever good enough for her."

"And you don't think that's reason enough for her to feel compelled to go on this date that her mother set up for her?"

I locked eyes with her, hearing what she was saying.

"Do you think that maybe you're feeling frustrated because Everly reminds you of your mom? Especially with what happened with her ex in his office?"

I looked away, the anger starting to build again.

"She's not her, Jared," she continued. "It's okay to want to protect her, but it won't change what happened to your mother."

"But she doesn't see the harm that she could be in," I muttered, pushing my hands together as I hung my head. "All it takes is one time for her ex to decide that he wants her again. Or some creep that stood her up to think that she owes him."

"That can happen to anyone at any time. You can't let this ruin your relationship with her."

"But she still went on that date, even after I confessed that I was falling for her and asked her not to."

"Because she didn't know how to tell her mother no. You can't blame her for not knowing how to stand up for herself with someone that has probably been doing this to her for her entire life."

 I sat up straight and looked at Shirley. I hated when she was right.

"Now go find her and fix this," she said with a smile. I got up and hugged her, holding her tight as I always did anytime I missed my mom a little more than usual. "And go buy her a present!"

"Okay, okay," I laughed. "I'm on it."

Nineteen

Everly

I was curled up on the couch wearing the same pajamas that I put on when I got home on Sunday. So what if I hadn't changed in two days? It wasn't like anyone was rushing over to see me on Christmas anyway. My parents were cruising through the Bahamas, and Becca was out of town with her family. Jared still wasn't talking to me, and aside from him, I didn't have anyone else to hang out with.

My tabletop tree was lit up, not doing anything to add any Christmas cheer to the room. The tv had been on a channel with non-stop Hallmark movies that were supposed to make you feel warm and fuzzy but instead, they just irritated me. If I still had the rest of the costume, I would be wearing the Old Man Grumpus outfit since it seemed to fit my mood.

I got up to use the bathroom and decided I might as well feed myself while I was up. It would be a few hours before I needed to go again and since showering and getting dressed weren't on my agenda, there wasn't anything else to worry about.

I went to the kitchen, dug a popcorn bag out of the pantry, and popped it in the microwave. It was better than nothing. There were wine bottles and empty ice cream cartons scattered along the counter by the sink, but I didn't have the energy to clean those up either.

As the kernels popped, I heard a knock on the door. I walked over and peeked through the peephole, gasping when I saw Jared on the other side.

"Open up, Everly. It's freaking cold out here," he said from the other side.

I ran a hand through my hair that hadn't been washed in days and grimaced at the thought of him seeing me like this.

"Um, I'm not feeling well," I lied. "Maybe you can come back another day?"

"Not going to happen, now please unlock the door."

I sighed, knowing that he would stay there all day if he had to.

I turned the locks and opened the door, holding my breath when a gust of wind came whipping past us.

He carried a handful of gift bags on one arm, filled with tissue paper poking out of the top of them. In the other hand, he had a brown paper bag with what smelled like food from somewhere.

"What are you doing?" I asked, stepping aside to let him in.

He walked over to the counter as I shut the door behind him.

"I came to talk to you," he said, busying himself with unpacking the food. "And, I brought dinner."

"You didn't have to do that."

I stayed standing where I was and watched him work effortlessly as he unpacked several to-go containers.

"I wanted to."

"Why?"

"Because," he said, finally turning to look at me. "I needed to say that I was sorry, and I was hoping that we could spend Christmas together."

He stepped toward me, placing his hands on my sides as I stayed frozen in place.

"Sorry for what?"

"For a lot of things," he sighed. "But most of all, for not listening when you wanted to talk about everything. I should have taken the time to hear you out, and I'm sorry that I didn't. I was angry and trying to process everything."

"I'm sorry too," I replied. "I should never have gone on that date, and I shouldn't have put myself in that position with Tom."

"I hated seeing you with him," he admitted. "It reminded me of my mom, and I lost it."

I nodded, understanding where he was coming from.

"I called Gail right after it happened and reported him. She called me back and let me know that I'll be in a new department starting Monday morning."

His eyes lit up as he squeezed me gently.

"I'm so proud of you," he said warmly.

"Thank you. And you were right about the date. It was terrible, and I should never have gone on it. I should have said no to my mother and told her that I was already seeing someone."

"Why didn't you tell her about me?" he asked, rubbing his thumb along my cheek.

"Because I was afraid that if I said it out loud that it would all end and you would just disappear. I didn't want to jinx it."

He gave me a small smile and pulled me in for a hug.

"At least you got a free meal out of it," he joked.

"Yeah, right," I snorted. "I ended up paying for the whole tab."

He pulled back and studied my face to see if I was joking. I shook my head and made a face.

"You have the worst luck with dates," he said with a laugh. "Hopefully, that's all over now?"

"Hopefully," I repeated, needing him to say it.

"If you're my girlfriend, then I would love it if you would stop dating other men and buying them dinner." I loved the way his lips turned up in the corners as he started to smile.

"Deal," I said, sticking my hand out to shake his. Instead, he grabbed it and pulled me back against his chest, holding me as if he was afraid to let go.

"Don't get too close," I warned. "I haven't showered in a day or two."

"Is that an invitation?" he asked playfully, wiggling his eyebrows.

"Maybe, but you have to feed me first," I said, ducking under his arm and rushing toward the food.

We grabbed the boxes from the counter and sat on the couch, diving right in. He had found a place serving Christmas dinner, which was something I hadn't had in a while with my parents traveling for almost every holiday.

We ate in silence, watching a love story unfold on the tv while we finished up. Finally, I set the empty container on the coffee table, ready to go take a shower.

"Wanna join me for some slippery, wet fun?" I asked, lifting the bottom of my hoodie and pulling it up my stomach.

"You bet your sweet ass I do," he growled. "But first, presents."

I let my hoodie fall back into place as I rushed into the bedroom and grabbed the gift bag I had waiting for him. When I went back into the living room, he was sitting on the couch with the bags he had brought in with him.

"Merry Christmas," I said, handing him the bag.

"Thank you, Merry Christmas to you," he replied, giving me my gift bags.

"You go first," he instructed, nodding to the two small bags in my lap.

"Does it matter which one I open first?"

He shook his head and watched me, his eyes sparkling.

I pulled the tissue paper out of the first one and dipped my fingers inside to pull out the small jewelry box. I looked at him then back to the box before I opened it. My fingers trembled slightly with excitement as they opened the lid.

Inside was a small Super Woman pin. I lifted it from the box and admired it.

"Sometimes, I know that you feel like you don't have the strength to do things," Jared explained. "But I wanted you to know that you are one of the strongest women that I know. Sometimes you just need a little reminder." He nodded to the pin and smiled.

"Thank you, this is so beautiful." I kept looking at it for a few seconds before placing it back in its box to keep it safe. I already had a few ideas of where I wanted to put it so I could see it every single day.

"Okay, now open the second one," he said excitedly, rubbing his hands together.

I laughed, pulling the tissue paper out of the other bag, and reached inside to pull out a larger box. There was no writing on it, so I opened it and found a smaller box inside. I covered my mouth as I looked at the picture of the vibrator on the outside packaging.

"Is this what I think it is?" I asked quietly, suddenly feeling shy.

"What do you think it is?" He pulled his lower lip in between his teeth. I loved when he did that.

"A massager?" I asked playfully, pretending not to know what it was.

"Oh, it's going to massage you, alright," he laughed.

I felt my cheeks flush as I set it on the couch beside me. It was Christmas, why not use my new present as soon as possible?

"Now it's your turn," I said, nodding to the gift in his lap.

He smiled and pulled the tissue paper out, laying it gently in his lap as he unwrapped each piece inside.

"Ties," he said with a grin.

"I couldn't help myself," I admitted. "After we played that game at brunch, I couldn't stop thinking of you touching my body with one. So I got you a handful to choose from."

"Thank you for the gift," he said, his voice suddenly husky. "Now, let's go use them."

He growled as he stood up and carried me to the bedroom with the ties and vibrator included as he got ready to make my Christmas wish come true.

Twenty

Everly

"Oh, right there," I moaned as Jared's tongue slid inside of me, parting my folds. "That feels amazing."

I arched my back, desperate to get closer to him as my orgasm crept up on me. My spine tingled as the blood rushed through my body, my breathing growing heavy with every second that passed.

He licked me lazily as if he had all the time in the world while I felt like I was going to explode against his face.

"I'm so close," I begged, shifting beneath him.

I felt him chuckle between my legs before he reached over and grabbed the vibrator lying beside us on the bed. I would have gotten it myself, but I was currently tied to the bed with one of the new ties that I had given him for Christmas.

A few seconds later, I heard it buzzing to life as he placed it against my clit.

"Ahhh!" I cried out, bucking my hips against his face.

He leaned back and scooted up to watch me as he slid it

inside of me, lining it up, so the flower at the end was hitting my clit perfectly.

I panted heavily, pulling against the silk tie as my body hummed with electricity.

"Open your eyes," he commanded softly.

I tried to force them to open, my body unable to concentrate on anything other than what was happening between my legs.

When I opened them, I found his dark green eyes locked onto mine, studying my face as my orgasm ripped through me. My body shook against the bed as he pressed the vibrator harder, pulling every last bit out of me.

"That was amazing," I panted, letting my body fall limp as he pulled the vibrator out then untied me. "By far the best Christmas present I've ever received."

He laid on his side and rested on his elbow as he laughed.

"That's not even all of your gift," he said with a dirty grin.

"What are you talking about?" I asked, rolling to look at him. "We opened our gifts before we came in here."

"Yeah, but I have one more for you. It's a surprise."

"A surprise?" My brows shot up, wondering what he was up to.

"Yes, now go get ready."

He patted the bed beside me a few times before getting up and walking out of the bedroom into the bathroom, butt naked.

"You better hurry," he called out as he turned on the shower.

I groaned, my body angry that I was forcing it to move. I followed him into the bathroom, stopping in my tracks as I looked at him through the glass shower door. He was face forward in the water as it ran down his body. His *gorgeous* body that I still hadn't had enough of.

"Mind if I join you?" I asked seductively, sliding the door open and stepping in.

"You know I like it when you're wet," he said as he stepped back to make room for me.

I stood under the hot water, feeling the heat of his gaze as he watched the water rush over my chest and down my breasts.

"I could fuck you all day long," he admitted, his voice gruff.

"Well, then, it's a good thing I don't have any plans today." I squirted some shower gel into my hands and lathered it slowly before rubbing it on my body, focusing on my breasts. My nipples hardened, and I felt the ache start between my legs again. There was no way that I would ever have my fill of him.

"Trust me, you don't want to miss what I have planned."

"Are you going to tell me what it is?" I prodded with a cheeky grin.

"Nope." He smacked his lips together and smiled back at me, knowing that it was getting to me that I didn't know what he had planned.

Half an hour later, we were both dressed and heading out the door. When we pulled up to what looked like an abandoned building with no windows and only one entry, I started to worry that maybe he had brought me here to kill me. There were other cars in the parking lot, but aside from those, there weren't any other businesses close by and no one to hear my cries for help if needed.

He parked close to the front entrance—if that's what you wanted to call it. It was hard to tell. Aside from the sign that read *Euphoria* hanging above the door, there wasn't anything else to indicate what kind of place this was. And it seemed funny that they would call this place *Euphoria* when it was painted black and looked dark and depressing.

"It'll be fun, I promise," he assured me, reaching over to squeeze my hand before getting out to come around and help me.

Before I could obsess about it, he was opening my door and extending his hand to help me down.

"What if I'm not dressed right?" I asked, suddenly nervous.

"Trust me, you're fine," he laughed lightly, his hand resting gently on my lower back as he glided me to the door.

I pulled at the short, black dress that barely covered my ass and regretted letting him talk me into wearing it. It was freaking cold outside, and I was about to freeze my ass off before he murdered me in this dark, gloomy parking lot.

We stood in front of the door, my teeth chattering involuntarily.

"Are you ready?" he asked, his hand on the handle.

I nodded and wrapped my arms around myself, trying to keep warm and calm my nerves.

He pulled the door open and stepped to the side, gently guiding me in with his hand on my lower back.

My jaw dropped open as I walked in, hearing the door shut behind us. The room was dark, like the outside, but dimly lit to cast a sexy glow throughout the room. We moved to the side to let a waitress past me, and I found myself turning to gawk at her.

"Is she…." I whispered, letting my voice trail off as I raised my eyebrows and nodded.

"Bodypaint," he answered, leading me to another room.

I felt in awe as I took everything in. The dark grey fabric of the chairs that were strategically arranged in the room to form a square with cocktail tables lined up in front of them, creating a smaller square. There was nothing on the table— just the clear, thin glass that allowed the perfect view of what was under the table, no matter where you were in the room.

Jared escorted me to one of the empty tables in the corner of the room, and we sat down. I looked around us, finding people scattered around—some couples and a few sitting by themselves. The lights were dim in this room as well, with music floating through the speakers above. It was loud enough to drown out the thoughts that were rushing through my head but not too loud to keep me from hearing the moans of the couple a few tables down.

I curiously peeked around Jared to see what was happening. He leaned back in his chair to give me a better view as his hand slid from my lower back to my ass.

My heart was racing as I leaned into him and tilted my head, getting a full view of the girl's legs spread wide as the guy next to her fingered her. Her lips parted as her head fell back, and she let another moan escape her lips.

I felt my breathing increase as I watched, wondering if they knew they had an audience.

"Euphoria is a club where people come to be watched or to watch others," Jared explained quietly in my ear, his hand still planted on my ass.

I turned my head slightly to look at him, not ready to take my eyes off of the other couple just yet.

"The tables are clear so you can see what they're doing underneath it. Some like you to watch them fuck, others like to masturbate. You can get pretty much whatever you're into."

I swallowed hard, watching as his fingers glistened in the light every time he pulled them back before plunging them back inside of her. I couldn't look away if I tried. I was fixated on watching this couple, who probably had no idea that I was looking at them.

Suddenly, the girl opened her eyes and locked onto mine. The seas of blue lit up beautifully in the light as a grin pulled across her face. Her lips were painted red, her tongue swiping slowly across them as she held my gaze.

She whispered something in his ear, causing him to look over at me. I felt Jared's body shift next to me, his chest hardening as he turned to watch them with me.

"They like you watching," he said low in my ear before gently nipping the lobe.

I nodded, unable to speak.

"Maybe he'll fuck her and let you watch," he suggested.

Instinctively, I reached my hand down and rubbed it across his cock. I could feel him getting hard and knew he was as turned on as I was.

The other couple continued to watch us as he fingered her for a few moments before whispering something in her ear. She bit the tip of her finger seductively and nodded. He pulled his fingers out and licked them, watching us the entire time.

She stood up, smiling at us before she turned to face him. He lifted her skirt, pushing it up to expose her bare ass before he reached down and unzipped his pants. A few seconds later, she stood with her legs parted, giving me the perfect view of his dick as it sprung free from his jeans. She smiled over her shoulder before stepping forward and straddling him.

Her heels were high enough to allow her to plant her feet on the floor as she lowered herself onto his dick, arching her back as she slid down. He looked over her shoulder, watching us as he grabbed her ass and guided her as she rode him.

With her skirt pushed out of the way, I could see his cock slipping in and out of her. I felt the wetness start to pool in my panties, knowing that I was completely turned on right now.

"Are you enjoying watching them fuck?" Jared asked as he kissed down the side of my neck.

I nodded, unable to speak as she started to fuck him faster. Her ass bounced perfectly as he held on. I panted in rhythm with them, feeling myself on the verge of needing a release. My body was ready and desperate to be touched.

"Can I get you something to drink?" a female's voice asked, startling me.

I jumped and whipped my head around. My heart raced against my chest, feeling like it was going to explode as I waited for it to get back to a normal pace.

"Sorry," she laughed, clutching her notepad to her chest as she looked sympathetically at me. "I didn't mean to startle you."

"It's her first time here," Jared explained, gently rubbing his hand on my back.

"Ahh," she said and grinned. "What do you think so far?"

"I'm not sure," I laughed nervously, feeling embarrassed that I had gotten caught.

"Trust me, you'll see and hear a lot in here. Nothing surprises us anymore." She waved dismissively as if people having sex in front of her was an everyday thing. Which, apparently, it was.

I pulled in a slow, steady breath, trying to calm myself. She was still standing in front of our table, watching as another couple started fucking on a table on the other side of the room. She frowned and shook her head.

"Give me a minute," she sighed. "I'll be right back."

She walked away, giving us a few minutes as she went to talk to them.

"You doing alright?" he asked, squeezing my hand a few times.

"Yeah," I breathed, finally calming down a little. "I wasn't expecting this at all."

"You mentioned that you might like to be watched when we had sex on the stage. So I thought this would be a good place to start. There's no pressure to do anything, and if you start to feel uncomfortable, we can leave."

"I don't want to leave," I quickly assured him. "Does that make me a pervert?"

He let his head fall back with laughter.

"You and everyone in here."

I felt the corners of my lips turn up into a smile.

A few minutes later, the waitress was heading our way again.

"Sorry about that," she apologized. "We have very few rules, but sex *on* the tables is one of them. The last thing anyone should want is a shard of glass cutting their ass when it breaks."

"Ouch," I shivered at the thought.

"Alright, so what can I get you guys to drink?"

"I'll have a glass of wine," I said. "A merlot if you have it."

She nodded and wrote it down before looking at Jared.

"Just water," he replied with a smile.

She nodded and tucked the pad under her arm before walking over to the next table to check on them.

"You didn't want anything to drink?" I asked.

He shook his head and wrapped his arm around my waist.

"I'm already fuzzy-headed from all of the blood in my body rushing to my dick, the last thing that I need right now is alcohol," he joked.

I laughed and leaned into him, feeling more relaxed being there. The couple next to us had finished while we were talking to the waitress and left. A new couple had taken the seats at the empty table next to where they had been sitting.

The room was getting fuller, but there were still plenty of empty seats around us, which allowed me to feel a little more hidden as I watched everyone else.

A few more waitresses made their way through the room, and I noticed that they all had the same body paint as the one I had seen when we first walked in.

"Are they elves?" I asked, nodding to the two that were heading our way. One was our waitress with our drinks, the other I hadn't seen before.

"They like to do themes," Jared shrugged.

"Here you go," the waitress said as she set my glass down next to his water. "If you guys need anything else, just let one of us know."

They both smiled before walking away.

"I almost had you wear the green leggings," he joked before taking a drink of water.

"I would have fit in with the theme," I agreed. "But it definitely wouldn't look as good as their body paint."

"We can make that happen. I have some paint at home."

I turned to find him grinning as he wiggled his eyebrows. I shook my head and smiled, leaning into him as we watched the people around us.

"Thank you for bringing me here," I said quietly.

"Thank you for trusting me. I knew that it was a risk, and you would either love it or hate it," he laughed. "But I thought, given the nature of our gifts earlier, it was fitting to keep with the theme."

I let out a slow, deep breath, thankful that my heart didn't feel like it was going to explode out of my chest anymore.

"I love it, almost as much as I love you."

He wrapped his arm around me and pulled me closer to him before whispering, "I love you too."

Twenty One

Jared

"That was amazing," I sighed, looking over at Everly.

"So amazing," she agreed, pulling the white sheet up to cover her body. "Do you think they'll get mad and come kick us out if we don't get dressed soon?"

"Well, it was a *one-hour* couple's massage, so probably."

"Ugh," she groaned, sitting up and throwing her legs over the side of the table. "I could've stayed there all day and fallen asleep."

"Me too," I laughed, getting up and letting the sheet fall on the table behind me. I grabbed my robe from the hook on the wall and turned around to find her standing there, watching me.

"You better be careful," I warned. "I have no problem going up front and seeing if they'll let me pay for another hour. This time *without* the masseuse."

"Well, then I guess it's a good thing that we already have a room."

"Dinner first," I growled.

While I was anxious to get back to the room and make love to her all night, I was starving—probably from our morning sex session—and ready to eat.

"Alright, alright," she joked, pulling the robe tight against her body. "Let's go get changed, and we'll head down to the steakhouse."

I nodded in relief and ushered her out of the room before she could change her mind.

We had spent the entire week together after Christmas. The night at *Euphoria* had changed things between us, and we found that we couldn't stay away from each other if we tried. We also went back a handful of times since then. For now, she was content with watching others and getting turned on before coming home and fucking my brains out. But I could tell that she was slowly getting more and more turned on by the idea of having someone else watch us.

I knew it was something she was interested in the first time we had sex, which was why I had taken her to the club, to begin with. I was relieved when she said that she liked it there and asked to go back. Each time she let me do something more than the time before, and just last night had let me finger her under the table while the waitress took our order.

We went up to our rooms and got ready. I called to confirm our reservation and smiled when they asked if we wanted to come earlier as they just had a cancelation. I quickly agreed and rushed Everly down there, loving the sound of her giggling along the way.

I watched as she ordered, smiling at the way she chewed her bottom lip as she tried to decide on which side she wanted with her steak. There were so many things that I loved about her that I hadn't noticed with other women before. At the end of the day, it felt like there was no one else in the world, but her and that was a place I wanted to spend forever.

****

Thank you so much for reading A Christmas Wish! I hope Everly and Jared gave you those warm, cozy holiday vibes we all crave this time of year!

If you're looking for more holiday romances, be sure to check these ones out:

Snow Place To Go (A small town, fake relationship)

https://books2read.com/u/4A560N

Chocolate Covered Mistletoe (Stone Creek Series, Book 1) (A small town friends to lovers)

https://books2read.com/u/3LRk9N

Other Books By Samantha Baca

<u>The Haven Brook Series:</u>

'Til Death Do Us Part (Haven Brook Book 1)

https://books2read.com/u/m2RJNR

The Cradle Will Fall (Haven Brook Book 2)

https://books2read.com/u/b6O0QE

The Ties That Bind (Haven Brook Book 3)

https://books2read.com/u/mqgoz8

A Very Haven Christmas (Haven Brook Book 4- Novella)

https://books2read.com/u/mvqGjj

Three Strikes, You're Gone (Haven Brook Book 5)

https://books2read.com/u/mvqL2z

<u>**The Dark Shadows Series**</u>

Five Steps Ahead (Dark Shadows Book 1)

https://books2read.com/u/38Q0gO

Ten Seconds Too Late (Dark Shadows Book 2)

Coming 2022

Against The Clock (Dark Shadows Book 3)

Coming 2023

Out Of Time (Dark Shadows Book 4)

Coming 2023

<u>**The Stone Creek Series (Novellas)**</u>

Chocolate Covered Mistletoe (Stone Creek Book 1)

https://books2read.com/u/3LRk9N

Candy Coated Promises (Stone Creek Book 2)

https://books2read.com/u/mldP5Y

Pumpkin Spiced Possibilities (Stone Creek Book 3)

https://books2read.com/u/bojdwV

<u>Standalone Books</u>

One Last Wish

https://books2read.com/u/mqg7D9

Finding Love In Apartment 2C (Novella)

https://books2read.com/u/bze9aZ

Cocky Counsel: A Hero Club Novel

https://bit.ly/CockyCounsel

<u>Holiday Books</u>

Snow Place To Go

https://books2read.com/u/4A560N

A Christmas Wish (coming 12/1/2021)

https://books2read.com/u/4EKXpE

Acknowledgements

First and foremost, I would like to thank the readers who took a chance on this holiday romance. Thank you for trusting me to entertain you for a little while, and hopefully, I was able to give you a nice escape if you needed one.

Thank you to my alpha readers—Chelsea and Azucena, for making the time in their hectic schedules to read this for me and give me their feedback. I appreciate you ladies, and can't imagine a book that we don't work on together!

To my beta readers—Camille and Amanda, you ladies really went the extra mile to read this when you knew that we had a tight deadline. Thank you for your speed reading and feedback to make it better! You're such a valuable part of my team.

Tillie, you never cease to amaze me with how selfless you are. Thank you for making the time to crank out the edits for this book and for getting it done in such a tight turnaround. I still owe you a pony, just let me know which one you want.

My dear, sweet husband, thank you for not divorcing me after I decided to go on this wild adventure that I didn't really have time for! I love how much you love and support me through all of my craziness! I couldn't ask for a better husband, father, and book formatter—you're the best!

To my girls, remember the joy of the holiday season and try not to make yourself crazy by creating projects that you don't have time for unless you have passion behind it. If you feel passionate about it, then you should ALWAYS go for it. Never let anyone tell you otherwise.

About the Author

Samantha lives in the southwest with her husband and two small children after abandoning her childhood dream of living in a cabin in Colorado when she found that she couldn't afford to live there and was deathly allergic to the woods. When she's not writing, she's usually spouting off sarcastic remarks while drinking wine out of a coffee mug to look like a functional adult while chasing down her toddlers. She enjoys spending time with her family, watching reruns of Friends, and the 24/7 flow of coffee that can be found in her veins. Be sure to follow her on social media for updates on what she's working on.

You can find her here:

Facebook: https://www.facebook.com/AuthorSamanthaBaca

Instagram: https://instagram.com/author_samantha_baca

Goodreads: http://www.goodreads.com/authorsamanthabaca

Facebook Reader Group:

https://www.facebook.com/groups/2945710968775398/

Webpage: https://authorsamanthabaca.wordpress.com

Newsletter: http://eepurl.com/g0NcSj